TIN WOODMAN

TIN WOODMAN

DAVID F. BISCHOFF AND DENNIS R. BAILEY

DOUBLEDAY & COMPANY, INC.

GARDEN CITY, NEW YORK

1979

All of the characters in this book
are fictitious, and any resemblance
to actual persons, living or dead,
is purely coincidental.

ISBN: 0-385-12785-5
Library of Congress Catalog Card Number 78-62599
Copyright © 1979 by David F. Bischoff and Dennis R. Bailey
All Rights Reserved
Printed in the United States of America
First Edition

*For Mary, Melanie,
and the Vicious Circle*

*And with special thanks
to Ted White, Sharon Jarvis,
Al Sarrantonio, and Pat LoBrutto*

TIN WOODMAN

PART ONE:

TO CALL THE DREAMER;
TO WAKE THE SLEEPER

> Below the thunders of the upper deep
> Far, far beneath in the abysmal sea,
> His ancient, dreamless, uninvaded sleep
> The Kraken sleepeth . . .

>   —Alfred, Lord Tennyson

>   THE KRAKEN

ONE

North America A.D. 2385

The man disliked these old Earth places. But the boy was here; it was best to talk to Div Harlthor in the environment to which he was accustomed.

The Institute for Exceptional Children was a complex of squat, domed, windowless buildings huddled together, hugging the earth within the confines of Old University Park. Like giant iron-boled trees thrusting up, concealing a forest clearing, the towers of the city rose beyond the perimeter of the park. Two kays eastward, the thousand-meter-high plasteel needle of the Control Tower marked the location of Phoenix Starport. On sunny mornings the daggerlike shadow of the tower's upper levels cut a black swath across the grassy quadrangle of the institute's mall. Generally, that specter was the only encroachment of the outside universe into the grounds and the affairs of the Old University complex.

The man considered this as he made his way across the grassy mall. It made him feel uneasy.

The role of intruder was not a part Assemblyman Bor Galvern thought he often played. With twenty years as chairman of the Committee of Territorial Exploration and Expansion, he had come to consider most of the known galaxy as part of his proper sphere of concern. Nonetheless, as he entered the office of Dr. Merton Severs, chief administrator of the institute, Galvern's professional aplomb was at a low ebb.

As Galvern met him, he observed that Dr. Severs shared certain characteristics with the institute he headed: smallness, neatness, colorlessness. His hair was short and tightly curled—a fashion ten years out of style, at least, as were the conservative gray business coveralls he wore. Severs was in unusual physical trim for a middle-aged city-dweller, however—a fact Galvern, a gray and grizzled old man of considerable bulk, noted with some envy. The doctor was apparently a man more concerned with function than appearance.

"I must admit that I had expected to be greeting most of your committee this morning," said Severs, after exchanging pleasantries with the assemblyman.

Galvern smiled uneasily. "Trips to Earth lend themselves to junketing," he joked. "Most of my colleagues won't be in a mood to conduct the public's business for at least another week. My personal aides are taking the grand tour of your facilities, in the company of one of your assistants."

The truth of the matter, Galvern knew, was that his fellow assemblymen had no more desire than he to make this call—the difference being that *they* had been given a choice.

Some disappointment evident in his demeanor, Severs laughed politely. "I quite understand. Well, then, we may as well proceed with the main reason for your visit. Any explanations or information I have to offer will be much more meaningful after you've met Div."

So saying, Severs led Galvern out of the administrative office bloc into the bare corridors and drab wardrooms which comprised the greater part of the institute. Here lived the many inmates for whom Severs and his staff cared. Galvern was interested in only one.

Div Harlthor.

When they finally reached his cubicle, Severs stopped, turned to Galvern. "I'm certain you're aware of the necessity for careful behavior in the presence of someone like Div," he cautioned. "Most particularly, at no time attempt to touch him."

Galvern nodded agreement absently. Severs thumbed the door buzzer, the door slid open, and they entered Div's room.

The young esper was reading, his spindly limbs poking up in an unaesthetic arrangement from behind a too-small desk. As Galvern and Severs approached him, Div glanced briefly up at them, his pink eyes startling in their size and depth. Galvern had the fugitive sensation of company inside his own skull.

"I'm sorry to disturb you, Div," Severs began mildly. "This is—"

"Assemblyman Galvern, of the Triunion Grand Assembly," the boy finished. He made no motion to welcome either of his visitors. He merely continued reading his book—*Finnegans Wake*, by James Joyce.

"His honor has come to Earth solely to see you," prompted Severs.

"I know. He might have used the one-way viewing wall. That's what it's there for."

"Yes, Div," Severs continued patiently, obviously used to the boy's recalcitrance. "I meant that he wished to speak with you."

"I *know*." Div shut his book reluctantly and turned his full attention to Galvern. With one pale, blue-veined hand, the telepath brushed his stiff red hair off his forehead.

A *nervous sort of gesture*, Galvern thought. Yet he could sense that Div was anything but nervous in his presence. "I presume you also know *why* I wish to talk with you," Galvern prodded.

"Of course. *Tin Woodman*. It consumes your thoughts," Div replied. "Save those concerned with your fear of me."

Galvern was shaken. "Look, son," he said, moving around behind Div's chair, fighting to stay calm. How did one deal with a Talent who knew every thought and feeling of everyone around him? Galvern knew very little about telepaths. But the government needed one—the best—and it had fallen to Galvern to find him.

Opting for a fatherly approach, Galvern reached out and placed a hand on the boy's shoulder. "No," Severs warned.

Too late.

An electric shock leaped up Galvern's arm, into his lungs. He pulled his hand away with a shriek.

"I'm sorry," Div said sincerely, "but that disturbs me. Dr. Severs should have warned you."

"I did," Severs muttered.

Angry and close to panic, Galvern groped for composure, tried to recover his dignity. "You are as adept as Dr. Severs promised." His voice was an unmodulated, rasping croak. He grinned with embarrassment. "I presume that you have already absorbed all that I know concerning the unknown discovered by the starship *Pegasus*?"

Div nodded. "None of your knowledge is very specific, however. If you intend for me to journey across space to deal with this—and I can see that this *is* your intention—I shall require all information on the discovery which has been relayed from the *Pegasus*."

Galvern was relieved. The request was surprisingly simple and straightforward. He reached into his tunic and produced a cassette. "This is designed to self-erase as it plays," Galvern explained, "so you'll only be able to view it once. When you arrive on board the *Pegasus*, however, you'll have ample opportunity to review the information it contains." He handed the recording to Div. "If you've no objection," Galvern continued, watching Div examine the cassette with interest, "we can put you on a self-piloting Mark IV messenger ship within two days. It will be outfitted with a Null-R drive, of course, and should rendezvous with the *Pegasus* in less than two weeks. I understand you've never been into space."

"No," replied Div. "I look forward to it." The confessional manner in which he said this caught Galvern off guard. Div spared him the necessity of replying by taking up his book again, his meaning unmistakable.

The audience was ended.

Div watched with relief as the two Normals exited. Neither could have been aware of how painful it had been for him, awash in the torrent of their emotional presences. They hated him, and he knew it.

I know them. I know them—and what do they think they're hiding? The thoughts came to his mind bearing the hot eruptions of emotions, the scalding, scarring waves of lava hate he had felt flowing over him from Normals. *Hide? From me? Hide the sun from a desert day? Hide water from a fish in the sea? I live in their thoughts when they're close like a thought-bird flying through the skies of their minds—and they pummel me with their hail of hate, their rain of suspicion, their chilling wind-driven snow of necessity. Yes, yes, oh yes, they need me now, need me even though they think me a freak, dangerous, able to turn their skulls to glass to see through into their private little doubts nightmares secrets kept half-buried. I'm a Talent—the best, or the most warped—too good to kill or Dope but damn it so unpredictable that maybe the needle in the brain would be a relief except they need me. Like my parents saying that I was a deliverance, come to prophesy, to deliver the sights of my mind into the primitive coinage of their words and they prayed but when I told them loving them what they were what I saw they hit me not with hands but with their minds—monster, monster son of Satan, creature of the depths, Legion, oh, they were afraid of my mirror mind holding up the looking glass to their natures. I am Dangerous because they don't understand that I mean no harm that I cannot help what I am that I am as human as they, that I need what humans need and without it I am—I am—I am a—*

Freak.

Div hurled his book against the wall and very quietly began to cry.

Galvern was immensely relieved to be back in Severs's office, away from Div. It read in the assemblyman's face. Severs grimaced sympathetically as he seated himself behind his desk. "I told you it would be rough," he said.

Galvern sank wearily into a recliner across from Severs. "I just hate making decisions about things I don't understand." He sighed. "Unfortunately, it's one of the responsibilities of public office. For my own satisfaction, I had to at least *meet* the boy before I made up my mind."

"I hope you found out whatever you wanted," said Severs. "I still have no idea what's going on. What is *Tin Woodman?*"

"That's classified information," Galvern replied, reaching into his waist pocket. "But I'm getting too old for this secrecy nonsense." He handed Severs a palm-sized vu-crystal. "This has a duplicate of the information on the tape I gave Div, in 3-D, though."

Severs snapped it into the video-field projector on his desk, twisted a dimmer knob which lessened the room's light, activated the crystal.

A holographic image of a star system appeared in the center of the room, occupying a cubic meter of empty air. It was a double system, composed of a golden yellow star in orbit around a much larger, rose-pink companion. Four planets were discernible, all gas giants. None of them appeared, on brief observation, to be habitable. "Aldebaran system," explained Galvern. "As the *Pegasus* first observed it. Edan Darsen in command."

Severs was startled. "Darsen? I thought he was—"

"Cashiered?" Galvern shook his head, somewhat embarrassed. "The Board of Review overturned the ruling on his court-martial. Came to the conclusion that the deaths on Goridan were technically not his command responsibility. They demoted him, gave him a nice safe assignment collecting stardust. Standard starship run—one of our big multi-purpose cruisers hauling colonists about, and simultaneously examining those very unfamiliar areas of space. I gave you the name, didn't I?"

"Yes. The *Pegasus.*"

"Right. Anyway, we made Darsen its captain. Just to keep him out of trouble."

"And he found some? Trouble, I mean."

"Perhaps. Excuse me—I've got to adjust the picture. Watch this."

With a shimmer, the magnification of the holograph increased. Now the main star nearly filled the viewing space. Near the star was a tiny dark object, orbiting the primary. Another shimmer, and the pin point of darkness resolved into an object—apparently a spacecraft of sorts, but matching no configuration that Severs had ever seen.

"Designated object *Tin Woodman*," Galvern announced.

"Why '*Tin Woodman*'?" Severs asked, still confused as to the significance of the artifact.

"It's from an old fairy tale. A man, made out of metal. Not a robot, but a living creature." Galvern relaxed visibly, obviously enjoying Severs's reaction. "There is no crew aboard *Tin Woodman* now, nor is it likely that there ever was. The ship itself is alive."

"Carbon-based life?" Severs asked, watching the holograph in awed fascination.

"Basically, yes," Galvern replied. "But the *Pegasus* has detected a structural latticework composed of metals, including steel, as well as synthetics. There are indications of a power generation unit capable of fueling a non-relative drive. And most important, there's a large, and highly organized, central nervous system." Galvern shook his head in mystification. "We don't know where it came from. We don't even know what keeps it alive. *Tin Woodman* is an enigma, to say the least."

Severs was silent for several moments. "You're absolutely certain of all this?" he asked at last.

"Absolutely," confirmed Galvern. "The *Pegasus'* crew spent two days taking and rechecking sensor and scanner data before relaying their report. And we had perfect reception of all messages and telemetry." He leaned forward toward the holograph and pointed at two dully pulsing metal globes embedded in the aft section of the ship-being. "These seem to be part of *Tin Woodman*'s propulsion system. We can't be certain, because the creature doesn't use them. Celestial mechanics hold it in orbit—it appears to be in some sort of torpor." Galvern shrugged, reaching across the desk to turn the projector off. "The rest of the record is full of graphs, mathematical analyses—you know, technical data.

"The problem is this: To all appearances, *Tin Woodman* represents a level of technological and engineering sophistication far in advance of ours. Yet we cannot communicate with it. It doesn't even seem to be aware of the *Pegasus'* presence. We therefore have no idea how long it has orbited Aldebaran, who built it—assuming it wasn't just spawned out there—nor any idea how intelligent it is."

Severs pondered this. "I don't imagine conventional translation devices would be much use in this situation. We can't have many literal concepts in common with a creature like this."

"Precisely," agreed Galvern. "The only means of communication the *Pegasus* crew hasn't attempted is telepathy. Direct mind-to-mind contact. So we need Div."

Severs drummed his fingers on the edge of his desk. "You saw him. You know he's anything but stable emotionally."

"Obviously," Galvern allowed. "There is some degree of uncertainty . . . of risk, both to Div, and to the discovery itself."

"You're due for the standard lecture on Talents, I think," said Severs grimly. "The gulf between our perceptual universe and that of the Talents is extraordinary in both quantity of sensory stimuli and the quality of that information. For example, in *our* early childhood, before we learn to erect barriers of custom and behavior between ourselves and others, natural barriers exist—our lack of fluency in communication, our inexperience, protect us. But Talents don't have that protection. They're exposed to adult anxieties, emotions, dilemmas, and frustrations from an early age. Complex thought patterns are forced on them, patterns which they can't understand or deal with. That so few of them survive to live a normal life is . . . well, predictable.

"Sometimes, a child who is only slightly telepathic will learn to control his Talent, to shut out the *noise* of outside thoughts. But Div is both a telepath *and* an empath. In the fifteen years that I've headed the institute, Div is the most sensitive case I've dealt with . . . or heard of. Contact with Normals is hell for him. Ordinarily, a case as extreme as his would have been Doped as a child."

"Doped?" Galvern's eyes grew vague, looking into memory. "You mean psyche . . . um . . ."

"Psychemicidian, yes. You see, Div's parents were Believers. When they found that their child was a Talent, they insisted they'd produced a prophet. They wouldn't authorize the treatments which would let him live a Normal's life. They carted him to revival meetings, made him do mental tricks—and worse. Imagine Div surrounded by the hopeful sick crying for a miracle, a healing.

"In a very real and terrible sense, Div was a battered child. When we finally won custody from the parents, the damage had been done." Severs's face became a study of disgust.

Galvern pursed his lips thoughtfully, obviously somewhat surprised at Severs's suddenly forceful, expressive demeanor. Some of the doctor's impassioned concern touched Galvern. *Perhaps the assembly could take more interest in these children than it did.* . . . "Couldn't you start the treatments now?"

Severs shook his head glumly. "You see, psychemicidian interferes with the functions of synapses in certain regions of the brain, effectively damping or destroying esper abilities. But as a side effect, it dulls the ego, blanks the personality of the individual. In an infant or small child, we can rebuild this through special education. But if the treatment is applied after the age of three or four . . . well, if you've never seen a Depressed esper, it's difficult to describe. Zombies." Severs's mind seemed to fix on the word. "Zombies," he repeated tonelessly and fell silent. Uncomfortable visions grew in Galvern's imagination as he dwelt upon the doctor's words.

"Well, there's nothing for it," Galvern said at last. "If Div is willing to take the risks, I have no choice. The *Pegasus* needs him." He rose from his seat. "The Tricouncil needs him."

"This is what I don't quite understand." As he walked with Galvern to the office door, Severs sighed. "Hold a moment . . . it just came to me. Shouldn't there be a Talent aboard the *Pegasus* already?"

"Of course," replied Galvern. "You're quite right—regulations require it. Designated as a shipman, or shiplady. Almost always a woman, you know." Galvern frowned. "The one of the *Pegasus* is, anyway. But frankly, Darsen claims she's completely unreliable. Her name is Elbrun. Mora Elbrun."

TWO

Article One

Every Service vessel of Cruiser class or heavier (i.e., any vessel of 200,000 gross tons displacement or greater) shall include as part of its standard crew complement, an Empathic Talent, to be designated Shiplady or Shipman.

Article Two

The Shiplady/Shipman shall hold the rank of Lieutenant in the Service Medical Corps.

Article Three

She/He shall have charge of monitoring the psycho-emotional extremes of officers assigned to the vessel's Command Crew, and is to determine and take steps to arrest the development of emotional instabilities among said officers during missions of extended duration.

Article Four

She/He is to accomplish the moderation of such emotional imbalances as may arise, through the use of empathic/telepathic stimuli, as any necessary physical therapy.

—Exerpted from
Triunion Space Service
Regulation Tapes
Spool 119034

Triunion Starship *Pegasus*
Aldebaran Star System

She lay paralyzed on her bed for several moments, tracing patterns on the darkened ceiling through half-closed eyes. The throbbing hum which had awakened her resolved slowly into a sourceless, monotonous buzzing. With a start, she realized that the noise was the access-control system of her cabin door. She dragged herself into a sitting position, waving her left hand clumsily over the room lighting panel. Wincing at the sudden brightness which flooded her tiny cubicle, Mora Elbrun punched the door intercom open. "Who—"

"Jin Tamner here. You wanna open the door? I've been leaning on the buzzer for ten—"

"Give me a minute," she groaned, cutting the line dead. Mora rose unsteadily, threw a short nightcape around her shoulders, signaled the door open.

Tamner sauntered in, a copy of the command duty roster in his left hand. Physically, he was a well-structured man. His face could even have been considered handsome, if one ignored the expressions it usually held. But to Mora, who interpreted individuals in terms of their personalities rather than their looks, he was not at all attractive on any level. The shock of smooth black hair to her was like a storm cloud settled atop his skull, flashing lightning bursts of self-involvement through cautious, ferret eyes. His nose was thin at the bridge but flaring at the nostrils; his teeth were even and white behind a sensuous mouth, which now smiled/scowled in perfect expression of the amusement, mixed with mean satisfaction, Mora could read in his mind.

"You shouldn't sleep with the intercom deactivated, Mora. You're on bridge duty," he said lightly. "Fifteen minutes late, in fact." The man stretched his angular limbs with exaggerated casualness, dropping the list onto a chair in front of her. He sat down on the edge of the bed.

Mora paced the room, shaking her head violently in a futile attempt to clear her mind. "Can't be so soon," she mumbled. "I was just relieved . . ." Her gaze fell upon the partly empty container of stress pills on her bunkside dresser. Tamner noticed them too, signaling his understanding with an unpleasant smile.

"Overworked, Mora?" he prodded.

Without warning, Mora felt waves of sexual desire—Tamner's, not her own—sweep through her. Still drowsy, caught off guard by the emotional and sensory assault, Mora staggered, nearly falling. Jin Tamner stood suddenly, reaching for her. . . . "How about a little physical therapy?" he said.

Mora hit him hard. Once.

Tamner released her and backed away, still smiling, though feelings of hatred and contempt still pulsed in his mind. No wounded pride, however. That stung Mora in a way which all his hatred could not.

How could she hurt *his* pride. She, who had none.

"Get out," she shouted, fighting off hysteria. "The next time you come here, you'd better have an EI from MedSec—" The feebleness of the protest embarrassed her. She watched silently as Tamner turned and left, the door sliding shut behind him with a hiss.

Mora slid down onto the bed, reaching into the top drawer of the dresser for her nausea tablets. She took three and reclined against the cool solidity of the cabin wall.

What a sadistic bastard, she thought, trying to dismiss the incident emotionally. Yet she knew that this was no good—Tamner was, for all intents and purposes, merely a little worse than other Normals, God protect her.

Slowly, she regained sufficient composure to dress for duty—blue uniform leotards, gold slacks and sleeveless jacket, quarter-length boots. On the left breast pocket of the jacket glittered the stylized silver star-and-caduceus of the Space Service Medical Corps. *It mocks me,* Mora thought as she arranged her long wheat-colored hair in a semblance of order. Reaching for the intercom, she punched out the code for MedSec.

"Ship's Medical Service—Psychological Testing Section. May I help you?" the contralto of Head Nurse Vandez responded.

"Shiplady Mora here. I overslept. I'll be down in about five minutes—"

"You'd best go straight to the bridge," interrupted Vandez. "The ship's still on a Class Two alert, because of *Tin Woodman.* Command has buzzed us twice already, looking for you."

Mora swore softly. This was unusual. Most of the command crew resented her presence on the bridge—Captain Darsen most of all. She had hoped to put off bridge duty for several hours. "No other assignments?" she asked.

"We have one mild depression, but we can handle her with drug therapy, I'm sure," Vandez replied smugly. "Oh, and one who needs your full treatment. To augment the psych-machine sessions we've been giving him. The doctor in charge suggested it might help. But the subject's not on active duty at the moment, so he can wait." Vandez paused. Mora could detect amusement in her voice, though her emotions were unreadable over the intercom circuit. "It's Scan Engineer Third Class Garth."

"Garth? Garth is the one who caused that scene last month about me. He hates even my shadow. He won't let me near him!" complained Mora.

"Subject will be in a state of sedation. Besides, he's important— command crew. Consider it a challenge."

"Damn!" She switched off the intercom angrily. *I'm a joke to them. Less than a person—a function of the ship. A biological mechanism.* Frustration welled up in her. She started to take two stress pills, thought better of it. Reluctantly, she signaled the door open and abandoned the shelter of her cabin, walking out into the cold corridors of the *Pegasus*.

Class Two alert aboard a starship called for overlapping shifts, resulting in unusually heavy traffic between decks and duty stations. Therefore, Mora was not surprised that she had to wait several minutes at the lift tube before a platform arrived that stopped on the bridge. When it finally did arrive, however, there was only one person on it—Leana Coffer, the *Pegasus'* executice officer. She smiled politely as Mora stepped onto the platform.

Leana Coffer was a native of Earth, but had spent much time on Crysor and Deva, the two planets which held an equal place with Earth in the Triunion, and therefore lacked a recognizable Earth accent. She was a small, thin, gray-haired woman—so thin, in fact, that her maroon-and-gold command uniform hung on her in deep folds, like a robe. Coffer, during her planetary travels, had assumed many of the finer qualities of the other two human races she had visited: discipline, tempered by a measure of humaneness. Mora respected this; of all the crew of the *Pegasus*, she could feel most comfortable in Leana Coffer's presence. Nevertheless, Coffer had an aloof quality, a faint preoccupied standoffishness in her character that Mora did not care to penetrate, for fear of discovering something ugly underneath.

"The specialist Darsen requested from Earth has arrived," Coffer said. Mora could read urgency, coupled with curiosity, behind the exec's words. "I was just on the hangar deck, inspecting the ship he came in." She frowned. "Do you know, they tacked a Null-R Field Generator onto an old, one-man mail carrier, and sent him in that? God knows what we're going to do with it—wretched shape, and we can't use many of its components. It sure won't get back; I'm surprised it made the trip at all. I guess we'll have to dump it—the extra mass isn't exactly good for our Null-R's." She shrugged. "I suppose they couldn't reroute a service vessel quickly enough to satisfy the brass. Still, they must have been desperate."

"Is he well?"

"Is who—oh, the specialist?" Coffer nodded. "Yes. Like I said, surprisingly the ship held up. I've not met him yet, but . . . I understand he's a Talent." Coffer hesitated a moment, seeing Mora's brightening. "I'd better warn you," she added, "that Darsen is still not pleased with that."

The platform finally reached the large, semi-circular room at the heart of the *Pegasus* from which all ship's operations were supervised —the bridge. Coffer, closely followed by Mora, strode off the platform and toward the wide, heavy metal instrument desk which was anchored against the back wall of the room. Mora felt her anxiety grow as they approached the console and the figure seated behind it whose huge, blond head was half engulfed by the lens element of a private tape-viewer. "Lieutenant Commander Coffer, reporting as ordered, sir," Coffer announced. Mora stood silently, nervously, a few paces behind the exec.

Darsen looked up from the viewer, waving Coffer a careless salute. His dark eyes were narrowed, the thin lips of his catfish mouth drawn tight against his teeth. Mora could read his emotions too clearly—a jumble of frustration, suspicion, and anger rising so strongly as to hamper his reason. Cautiously, Mora moved toward him. *This is my duty,* she thought. *This is part of the reason I'm aboard this ship.* Yet she was frightened, far more frightened by Darsen than by anyone else aboard the *Pegasus.*

Tentatively, unobtrusively, Mora placed a hand on Darsen's shoulder. Within, she strove to banish fear from her mind—to find an island of calm, the deep center of her being which the academy had attempted to train to this purpose. Cool, soothing images, which Mora tried to communicate to Darsen's unconscious . . .

Edan Darsen shrugged the shiplady's hand away with a wave of emotional repulsion which knotted Mora's stomach. With a small cry, she stumbled to the sanctuary of her Museplace, activating its pitiful, almost useless yet helpful Damper field. Inside the small, dark alcove located in the wall a few paces from Darsen's desk, slightly protected from the emotions of others by a screen of energy which scrambled them, she felt her fear taper away into something she could handle.

And yet Mora hated the dull, partially blind sensation which restriction of her empathic Talent always produced. The soft darkness of the Museplace offered her a temporary shield of sorts, but little solace.

"Listen to this," Mora heard Darsen growl as he placed his head back to the view. "Name: Divam Gelon Harlthor. Age: Nineteen years, Earth Standard. Ancestry: Human, Earth. Telepathy/Empathy Quotient: Broad-range, beyond practical measurement. Resultant Psycho-emotional Instability: Upper range of uncertainty . . ." Darsen halted suddenly, standing and slamming a beefy hand down to deactivate the viewer. "I don't believe it. They've sent us a goddamned kid."

Coffer laughed unsympathetically. "That isn't what you object to," she said, crossing her arms as she advanced toward Darsen. "You simply cannot stand Talents. Admit it. You'd ship Mora out tomorrow if service regulations didn't require a ship-person aboard."

God, thought Mora. *They act like I'm deaf and blind in here.* She had stood mutely through many similar disagreements, listening from her Museplace, and it seemed to her as if the Normals *did* somehow forget that she was present.

"It doesn't make any sense," Darsen said, "that with the technology and resources the Tricouncil can draw on, they place as much emphasis on *espers.*" From Darsen's lips, the name sounded like a snake's hiss. "Most of them are half-crazed, and damn useless to boot."

Coffer opened her mouth to argue, but was interrupted by a shout from across the room. "Captain! Ship's sensors are picking up changes in *Tin Woodman's* energy output." The voice belonged to Lieutenant Genson, a short, intense woman seated at the bridge's main sensor scan station.

Darsen brushed past Coffer, striding over to look at the flat-screen displays on Genson's consoles. He shot a question back at Lieutenant Norlan, the chief communications officer. "Picking anything up on your channels, Mr. Norlan?"

Not bothering to lift his head from his control banks, Norlan answered: "Nothing new here, Captain."

Obviously frustrated in her own attempt to communicate, Coffer moved alongside Darsen. But Mora hesitated, her curiosity struggling with her fear of the captain. Finally, she abandoned her Museplace and went to stand with the others.

Darsen surveyed the graphs and tables which flickered brightly on the screens. His already choleric temper seemed to blacken further; Mora's only reaction this time was to throw up what mental barriers she could against his emotional energy. "My God, look at that!" Darsen exclaimed to Coffer. "Half a dozen radiation readings have zoomed practically off the scale!"

"Field Generators of some kind," Coffer observed. "We've been watching it for three weeks now, and this is the first—"

"We have no way of understanding that thing." Darsen's gaze swept the bridge, fixing on Mora as if she were somehow responsible. "*Something* has wakened *Tin Woodman,* and all we can send against it is a nineteen-year-old boy."

THREE

Freedom, Div thought. *Freedom from the oppressive cold cloister of walls.* Looking out through the transparent, filtering dome of the *Pegasus'* observation deck, Div watched the twin stars of the Aldebaran system and imagined that he could see the tiny island of life which had brought him here—*Tin Woodman.* Closing his eyes, he could see it clearly, as it had appeared on Galvern's holographs. He saw the long, slender ovoid, glistening silver in the radiation of the great nuclear lights—not the hard, glinting silver of steel, but the rainbow-faceted gleam of a rare and beautiful fish.

So intent was Div upon this image that, for the first time in his life, other humans approached without his immediate awareness.

"I suppose it *is* awesome, when you're not used to it," a gravel-edged voice from behind Div said. The young Talent spun around, his heart racing, as if expecting attack. Willfully, he forced himself to appear calm.

"How can one become used to it?" Div replied, his voice quavering.

The intruder dismissed the question with a shrug. "I'm Edan Darsen," he said, then began to introduce his two companions. Recovering from his initial shock, Div superficially scanned all three minds.

From Edan Darsen and Leana Coffer, he received mainly those feelings he had come routinely to associate with Normals: apprehension, defensive and useless guarding and dissembling; an offensive let's-get-it-over-with-and-get-away-from-him underlying attitude. Darsen's thoughts were tinged with something more frightening—a hatred for Talents which threatened at a moment's notice to boil over and scald his thinking. Div fought to block all this out.

The woman in the medic's uniform was different, however. She was a Talent, a fact Div could have ascertained without using his own powers. It was clear in the peculiar *listening* way that she held her head, as well as the indefinably drawn and melancholic lines of her attractive face. An aura of constant nervous agitation, apparent even to a Normal, surrounded her slim, almost angular figure. But, above all, her nature was evident in her eyes. They were like his own, a size too large for her face, and lacking any pigmentation. Pale orbs, which Div had come to think of as bleached—scorched color- less by the process of taking in so much more of the world than Nor- mals. Div touched her mind only momentarily, seeking the reassur- ance of a chance meeting with another of his kind.

But he could sense no reaching-out from her. She seemed very careful; aloof.

"You were briefed on the situation before leaving Earth?" Darsen asked Div. Div nodded rather distantly, attention still on Mora. It seemed to annoy Darsen. "*Tin Woodman* is over two hundred me- ters in length," he said hoarsely, "and to all appearances is a living creature. Degree of its intelligence is still undetermined. Our sensor data indicate that its stardrive and energy sources are highly sophis- ticated, far in advance of anything the Triunion possesses.

"In addition, there's been a change in the situation since you first arrived. *Tin Woodman* seems to be coming out of its fugue. It still doesn't acknowledge our existence, but its utilization of power is in- creasing throughout its systems."

Div's expression didn't change. "How does that affect what you want me to do?"

The boy's apparent confidence left Darsen nonplused. "It in- tensifies the urgency of your mission," he snapped. "I want you to communicate with the thing. Persuade it, if possible, to follow us to our next port of call, where it can be properly subjected to study and experimentation." Darsen drew up to his full height, attempting a dignified demeanor. "I don't want anything to go wrong now. This could be the most important First Contact in the history of the Triunion."

Important in the history of Edan Darsen. You want your name cleared. You want the fame of discovery. Div picked the thoughts ac- cidently from Leana Coffer's mind, amid strong currents of disdain for Darsen.

"Are you paying attention, boy?" demanded Darsen in exasper- ation. Div frowned slightly, trying to refocus his eyes on the pom- pous man. *You're asking me to commit a cosmic sin,* he thought angrily. He became abruptly aware of another presence in his mind. Mora was scanning him. She gave no indication to either Darsen or Coffer of what Div was feeling.

"I'm simply tired, sir," Div replied at last. "Disoriented . . . this is my first trip through space." Darsen seemed satisfied with that. Div knew that the captain expected rather bizarre behavior from Talents. "There's nothing I can do from this distance," he continued, his voice steady, his tone firm. "I need to get much closer to *Tin Woodman* in order to attempt telepathic communication."

Darsen didn't hide his dislike for this idea, but he had no real alternative but to co-operate. "Very well," he agreed. "You can use one of our robot-piloted Spiders. We use them for hull maintenance, and emergency transport between spacecraft. You'll go alone—no sense in risking more than one person. I'll take the *Pegasus* in as close to the alien as I judge safe. From there, you're on your own."

"Thank you, sir," said Div. "I'm sure that will do quite well. Now, I'd like to rest awhile."

Darsen grunted. "You have eight hours in which to do so. With *Tin Woodman* behaving unpredictably, we can't afford to wait any longer." Darsen turned to Mora, not looking directly at her. "See that Mr. Harlthor is made comfortable. Check with Accommodations. They should have a spare bed someplace for him to rest on." With that, Darsen spun on his heel and retreated from the room as quickly as dignity would allow. The exec smiled awkwardly at Mora and Div, then followed Darsen.

Div and Mora were alone.

Some of the tension drained from her mind with Darsen's departure.

Some. Not all.

She led him to the lift shaft and programmed it for one of the crew quarters decks. Div stepped onto the platform with her and the lift started with a slight lurch. The air smelled faintly of electricity.

"They've probably got you a cot by the bilge pump," Mora joked awkwardly, grimly. "Our captain doesn't care much for our sort." She stared at him hesitantly. His face remained set in the impassive lines it had worn during his entire meeting with Darsen. "You are not what I was told you were," said Mora. She realized she was fingering the left cuff of her jacket nervously.

"You were told," Div said casually, "that I'm unbalanced. That they plucked me out of a sanitarium on Earth. That they picked me because no sane human being would volunteer to endure two weeks of non-relative space, alone."

Mora nodded.

"It's true," Div said simply.

Here's an enigma, she thought. She had scanned the boy earlier. She knew that he had fear and panic and anger packed into a tight light ball inside himself. He was trying to win a game, with the Normals and with himself. The same game that Mora had been losing for a long time.

"You should understand," said Div. "I know how you feel here."

Mora, on sudden impulse, dropped the shield from her thoughts. *You couldn't possibly. I'm a failure. A miserable shiplady. If I weren't, Darsen wouldn't have sent for you.*

Just what are you failing at? Div demanded. He was thought-casting, an unusual experience for Mora, who was accustomed merely to receiving emotional readings. *I'm not sheltered, nor naïve, Mora. They couldn't build walls thick enough on Earth to allow me that luxury. Four years in the service academy couldn't persuade you of the nobility of your sort of prostitution. Who failed?*

Very perceptive. Mora was at once sorry for the bitterness behind the thought. Div was like her. That his impressions of her, based on ten minutes' acquaintance, were somewhat superficial hardly merited her scorn.

Div reached out and took her arm. His eyes met hers, and he opened his mind to her, totally. Mora recoiled under the bombardment of images, feelings, and thoughts which flooded her consciousness. Even as she did so, she realized that Div was forcing nothing on her. She had merely to will it, and the flood ceased at once. Shutting him out, Mora was safe in the silence of her mind.

But she opened her mind again. Trusting Div now, she let him see into her own soul. She let him see the fear, the vulnerability which Normals always seemed to sense. Since childhood they'd abused her, stabbing into her mind to relieve their own pain. As she had grown into womanhood, men became the worst, deadliest of vultures with their sadism-passing-virility pounding pounding pounding on her soul until she thought she—

So, Space Service was my last refuge, Mora thought, suddenly compressing and organizing her thoughts and assigning them words. *I had tried . . . I'd moved around. I'd tried to live in the little farms and villages—Schuylkill Haven, Willowood—where Talents live apart, building their own worlds. But I felt as though I were*

*running. The world that mattered, that I knew, was outside, allow-
ing us to do this.*

*They call us Talents and laugh. They mock us. They call us
Talents and then can't decide to cure us or kill us. Because they
know all we really are is disturbed. Unbalanced and dangerous.
But when I was a child, I didn't understand the laughing. They
called me a Talent and I believed it. I felt I should use my "gift" to
help others.*

*So I came to the service. What human beings were doing in
space was noble—surely such people were too disciplined, too re-
spectful of one another to waste energy on the luxuries of torture.
I went to the academy. I spent four years trying to learn the mental discipline, the little tricks a shiplady has to know. I learned the
soothing ways of "physical therapy" and a lot of other nonsense—
all their excuse for sticking me here to whore in a little metal can
falling through space, where people are only people after all. . . .*

Mora let the train of thought fade as she tottered there on the
brink of night. She looked at Div. There was no pity in his eyes. Instead, there was understanding. And the beginnings of something
deeper. Their clasped hands tightened together.

"Would you like some coffee? We can take it to my cabin," she
said aloud as the lift platform came to a halt on Mora's deck.

Div said, "Something else besides coffee, maybe."

She gave him a trembling smile and led him to a drink station.

RAC COMMUNICATIONS, INC.
MAGNEPAPER®   #TX8794a

Leana Coffer
Exec. Commander
Triunion Starship PEGASUS

Dear Me,

Vocoder time again.

Met the Talent from Earth. Div Harlthor. He worries me. Reminds me
of Mora Elbrun—without Elbrun's strength. Odd. Never thought of Mora
as a woman with a strong character. Compared to this boy-freak she seems
sturdy as a soldier in combat armor. Harlthor was confined to a sanitarium
on Earth, and seeing what the Talent can *do* to a human being I rather

wonder at the inner reserves Mora must have to exist in the hostile world of this ship.

This ship. Darsen's little world. Another reason Harlthor worries me. I know what Darsen wants—and why—though I don't think he knows himself. He's not analytical but emotionally driven and on the *Pegasus* his needs become commands and are translated into obedience so quickly that he need never define, measure, or control them. I can see what the man's ideals are: entirely egocentric, a puffing up of self. Darsen's damned selfish, and I'm sure this fact has not escaped Harlthor. I just can't see their intentions or modes of approach toward the alien as compatible at all. Darsen's reasons are entirely personal—but I can't fathom Div Harlthor's yet. If this perception is correct, why is Darsen giving the Talent such power?

Of course, the captain hasn't thought this through. He's incapable of that. He needs a personal triumph so badly that he can't conceive of his need being frustrated—certainly not by a boy whom he holds in such obvious contempt. To Darsen, Harlthor must be a piece of equipment, a robot to be powered by his will, to be ordered about and used and possibly sacrificed for an objective—just as that minor megalomaniac must have viewed his soldiers in that battle on Goridan.

I think I'm making sense. But I'm not an uninvolved observer, and may be projecting my feelings on to the situation more than I like to admit. I can't forget my horror—no, anger—when I learned that Darsen was to be the new commander of *Pegasus*. It's useless to pretend to myself that experience and time have changed my belief that I should have been given command. I still wonder what kind of system gives a man like Darsen a second chance after a disaster like the Goridan massacre. Someone in the high councils of the service, far beyond the levels of Darsen's personal influence, saved his career for him. Well, maybe it fits in with my theory. . . .

Mora lounged in her chair, watching Div, who lay on her bunk in a semi-somnambulent condition, his breathing slow and quiet. There had been much to discuss, and they had done so exhaustively, with minds and mouths. Realizing that not much time was left, Mora had insisted that Div rest on her bunk. No time to see about your quarters, she claimed. And Div had not objected.

She sat now, content to watch him rest, to feel his presence. Delicately, she let her mind attempt to lull his into deeper sleep.

A GLIMPSE OF RAINBOW DAWN THROUGH THE MIST OF A METHANE WORLD. WHIRLING VORTEX DROPLETS OF AMMONIA ICE CLINGING TO HULL . . . THE BURNING RAIN WHICH KILLS . . . VUL. DEATH. ALONE. EMPTINESS.

COME . . . YOU HAVE COME . . . WELCOME . . .

"Div!" Mora cried out inadvertently, stiffening. The alien sensation passed. Div tried to sit upright abruptly, as if in terror. Mora stood, trying to ease him back. "What was that?" she asked, afraid of the answer she already knew.

"*Tin Woodman*," Div replied. He lay back again, clutching onto Mora with something like frenzy. Struggling to understand the impressions she had accidentally glimpsed, Mora realized that they had been hidden in Div's mind all the time.

"You're already in contact with it, then?"

Div stared at the ceiling for a moment, then turned to her, holding her eyes with his.

"Yes, I caused it to wake."

Later, Div asked, "How long? Before I have to go out there, I mean?"

"About two hours," she said.

"I can't sleep. I'm going to go back to the observation deck, to see it again, to be *closer*." His sudden vehemence frightened her. He jerked up from the bed to his feet.

"Do you have to?" she asked.

"You can come with me, if you like. Please do."

"No," she whispered. "I can't. There are bound to be other people up there. I don't want to face them so soon. I need time to think. No, I *won't!*" She looked at Div desperately as he opened the cabin door. He turned back to her, silhouetted in the blue light of the corridor beyond.

I know, he cast gently. *I wish I didn't love them, too.*

FOUR

Leana Coffer sat at the bridge's launch monitor, running through a last check of the hangar deck's subsystem's display. "Hangar depressurized," she reported, turning away from her console to face Darsen at his command station. "Bay doors are powered up, and robot guidance on the spider checks out normal."

Glumly drumming his fingers along the edge of his desk, Darsen acknowledged the report.

"We can proceed with launch on your command, Captain," finished Coffer.

"Activate the spider's inboard monitor now," Darsen ordered, gesturing toward the globe of the bridge's main vu-tank. "I want to keep an eye on the boy. Don't trust him at all."

"Why?" asked Coffer. "What could he do?"

"I'm not sure," muttered Darsen. "But Harlthor hasn't been playing straight with us. I know it."

Coffer shrugged and activated the vu-tank. A holographic image of the hangar deck, transmitted through the *Pegasus'* internal surveillance cameras, coalesced within the huge crystal globe which hung suspended in the center of the bridge. The vu-tank showed the dull gray bulkheads and sharp black shadows of the hangar deck. In the middle of the picture, centered over the bay doors, stood the spider. The craft rested on six of its eight articulated metal appendages. The remaining two thrust forward into the air, their grappling claws extended. The cabin of the craft was nothing more than an open metal cage with a seat bolted into it, mounted just below the point where the legs joined the body of the ship. Gilt metal shielding separated the cabin from the chemical engines which propelled the spider. Exposed cables ran up and down every surface.

Coffer switched over to the spider's inboard monitor; the scene in the vu-tank dissolved into a close-up of Div's head, his features hidden behind the dark visor of his reflective yellow pressure suit. Darsen stared at the image as though trying to pierce the black mirror of Div's helmet and read the boy's expression. After several moments, the captain returned his attention to Coffer. "Okay. Proceed with launch when ready—signal that to the local controller," he ordered. "And keep that monitor on." He looked around the bridge realizing that someone was missing. "Where the devil is the shiplady?"

"Do you care?" asked Coffer, coldly.

"Not really. Log her as absent from her post."

Darsen watched the vu-tank sullenly.

Mora stood alone in one of the observation rooms which lined the walls of the hangar deck, separated from the depressurized launch area by less than an inch of transparent metal and plastics. She made no attempt to reach out to the mind of the boy who sat strapped into the heart of the spider. She knew that Div's thoughts were fifty thousand kays distant, focused on *Tin Woodman.*

The door behind her slid open. A young man wearing an engineering uniform entered the observation room. She read him, found that he was surprised that the room was occupied. Nothing more. She had never noticed him before; he did not appear to recognize her.

"I'm supposed to watch the launch," he said, smiling. "Do you mind?" Mora shook her head. As he walked across the room toward the mirror next to her, she saw that he was no taller than herself, well under two meters tall. His hair was dark, his eyes were brown; she guessed from his features that he was a native of Earth, probably of European ancestry. He wore an ensign's badges on his flame-colored uniform. And he was certainly young—perhaps twenty-three years old.

"My name's Ston," he offered. "Ston Maurtan."

"I'm Mora . . . Elbrun," she replied, trying to watch the hangar deck without being impolite. Ston did not seem to recognize the name.

"I've been aboard about three months," said Ston. "Just commissioned. I'm really still in training—the Chief Engineer said I should observe this." Maurtan smiled again. He seemed loquacious, but was so unaffectedly friendly that she didn't find him annoying.

Suddenly the warning lights which lined the bay doors of the hangar deck flashed red. The doors began to part beneath Div's vehicle. Mora's attention was drawn back to the launch.

"That's the telepath from Earth, right?" asked Ston.

Mora nodded absently, intent on the event unfolding beneath them. A tingling crawled up her spine. A sense of dread, and yet at the same time a sense of giddy elation. Then she realized that Ston was gazing at her as intensely as she had been staring at the ship. She looked him in the eyes, then self-consciously turned back to peer downward.

"What's happening here?" asked Ston, slowly. "Something more than meets the eye, I think." His tone was not stern; merely inquiring. The emotional waves Mora received from him were calm, concerned.

"No—just what you see," said Mora in a strained voice. "Just what we've waited these weeks for. A Talent to make contact with *Tin Woodman*." Even as she spoke, she chastised herself. There was nothing to fear from this young man. And yet she could not help but act defensively, the response was so ingrained in her in dealing with Normals.

"You're a Talent too, aren't you?" said Ston.

Mora, startled, pivoted toward him. How did he know? She had donned her civilian clothes for this—she felt more anonymous. And she'd slipped on blue contact lenses over her telltale eyes.

"How—how do you know?"

Ston Maurtan smiled slightly. "Oh, different things. The guarded way you stand, as though someone might strike you at any moment. The way you hold your head. The way your hands move. In fact you remind me of—" A troubled look crossed his features; Mora felt a flutter of pain from his emotion-mix. "No. Let's just say I know, and be done with it." He placed a hand on her wrist. Now his face was full of understanding. "Yes. You needn't tell me, but I think there's much more happening here than I can see." He glanced down at the departing spider. "Much more."

Ston kept silent, hoping that Mora would offer some comment to his statement. But she did not.

Her thoughts seemed to turn inward. Her eyes turned back to the boy in the spider. The thoughtful, troubled expression on her face was startlingly familiar to Ston.

He was reminded of his sister Adria. His memories of her were painful ones, yet precious to him. She had been a Talent, like Mora, and Mora's resemblance to her aroused some protective instinct in him. He tried to shrug the feeling off—he hardly knew this woman.

She seemed pleasant enough, but . . . It was no use. The more he sought out the differences between Mora and his sister, the deeper their similarities seemed to insinuate themselves into his mind. It was an eerie feeling—and a lonely one.

Whatever inner anguish caused the shiplady to watch Div Harlthor in such a troubled way, Ston wanted to help her.

The hangar doors slid away under the spider.

Its retro rockets thrust the ship away from the artificial gravity field of the *Pegasus.*

Then Div was weightless. He could see the *Pegasus* tumbling away above, then behind him. He knew that to an observer aboard the starship, it was the spider which appeared to be spinning aimlessly away. After a minute, the retro mobility rockets died, and the robot pilot fired the spider's main engine. Div felt a sensation of weight again as the considerable thrust pushed him back in his seat.

He was moving in a direction counter to that of *Tin Woodman* and the *Pegasus,* moving toward the former along the path of the alien's own orbit. Somewhat under fifty thousand kilometers in the distance, *Tin Woodman* was rushing toward him.

Again, Div was in space, alone, out of range of the interminable noise, the constant dull roar of people loving, fighting, hating, *living* with a passion he had never dared. Ahead, guiding him now, the single placid being known only as *Tin Woodman* seemed to expand, big as fate. Seemed to envelope his mind, like the blooming of a rose.

The many minutes passed slowly.

Finally, the spider ship's pilot went into a braking maneuver, reacting to the appearance of the alien on its short-range sensors. All sensation of motion disappeared as Div's craft matched speed and trajectory with that of *Tin Woodman.* Now, the alien was finally visible to Div himself, appearing as a silver light which grew larger and brighter as it approached.

Pacing the alien, a few kilometers away and closing rapidly, Div felt as if he were hanging motionless in the void. Everything important in his universe depended upon his actions in the next few minutes. He twisted his head to the left, peering into the lens of the spider's inboard monitor. Darsen was watching him. No doubt about that.

Bolted underneath the seat was a tool kit, intended for minor maintenance on the vehicle. Cautiously, watching the monitor, Div reached down, opened it. He ducked his head downward to examine its contents. The monitor swiveled to follow his movement.

There was no way, then, to disable the monitor without being seen.

He would have to use a quicker method.

There was a large wrench inside the box. He unstrapped it, grasping it by one end. In full view of the monitor, he brought it up above his head.

Div drove the wrench into the monitor lens, smashing it. He released the tool, and it spun off into space, amid many tiny shards of lens crystal. He hit the button that released his seat straps. Free of these, out of Darsen's sight, he pulled himself out of the cage and thrust out into space.

As Mora stepped off the lift platform onto the command deck of the bridge, she saw Edan Darsen staring disbelievingly into the empty grayness of the main vu-tank.

His fury hit her mind like a bomb blast.

"The bastard's put out the monitor," he cried. "Switch to the outboard monitor, fast. I'm going to override the robot." He flipped the switch causing the remote shuttle controls to rise from concealment within his command console.

Mora could read his emotions. There was murder in his mind, clear and unmistakable.

"What do you intend to do?" demanded Coffer as she rose from her station.

Darsen ignored the question. "Just get me that other monitor," he snapped. "I can't get him if I can't see him."

Mora watched Darsen in horror for several moments. Then she began to walk toward him across the bridge.

The vu-tank came alive suddenly, focused on *Tin Woodman*. The spider was quite close to the creature. Close enough to allow a human figure in a bright yellow pressure suit to be seen drifting along the side of the alien, gloved hand pressed lightly against the living tissue of the hull, as if caressing it. Near Div, an opening was forming in the substance—*Tin Woodman*'s flesh drawing back like the iris of a human eye.

There was no mistaking Div's intention. He was going to enter *Tin Woodman*.

Mora noted all this mechanically as she circled the vu-tank suspended in the center of the bridge, moving toward Darsen. She watched as the metal claws of the spider rose up close in the foreground of the holographic image, then extended toward *Tin Woodman*. Under Darsen's command, the spider was moving in on Div rapidly.

As Mora approached Darsen, she saw the deft, cold-blooded way in which he manipulated the spider.

It frightened her.

She felt the hatred and anger which raged in his mind. But she was not confused or hesitant. She felt clearheaded. She knew exactly what she was going to do. What she *had* to do.

Mora locked her right hand around Darsen's left wrist. She drove her mind, knifelike, into his mind.

Screaming, Darsen leaped out of his chair, away from the console.

Mora did not release him. Instead, she probed deeper, feeling no sympathy; only the echoes of Darsen's pain through her empathic faculties.

"Look at me," she demanded.

Darsen angled his face upward, eyes bulging. He gasped for breath, his hand grabbing futilely at his head, as though to break the link with Mora through physical force.

Mora forced him to his knees.

"Look at yourself," she shouted, making her mind a mirror. All the hatred, the fear of Darsen rose to the surface. "Look at the horror, at the pain you've caused. Look at yourself as another sees you!"

Darsen shrieked.

He was trying to speak, but his words were inconsequential to her. He lunged, grabbing her throat with his free right hand.

In defense, Mora fought back with her mind, losing control.

Instantly Darsen arched back, wide-eyed, hair wildly disheveled, as if struck by a high-voltage electrical cable.

Mora released his wrist, and he crumpled to the floor, spasming feebly.

She gazed about the bridge. The crew had ceased their activities, but no one moved toward her. They had simply watched it all, motionless, afraid to interfere.

Mora checked the vu-tank.

Div had disappeared from the picture. The doorway in *Tin Woodman*'s hull was sealed.

Darsen was hurried to MedSec—alive, but unconscious.

Leana Coffer felt ill. So this was the sacrificial victim of both Darsen *and* Harlthor. Poor Mora Elbrun. She had to set the security guards upon her of course. Now they walked—cautiously after the display of Mora's previously unknown power—from the lift shaft, their stunners drawn.

Somehow Harlthor had gotten this woman to cover him, thought Coffer, knowing the action he would take, and the response it would invoke from Darsen. But how, and why—and what was Harlthor doing inside the alien now? But her duty rapidly shoved aside these speculative thoughts—she was in command now.

Mora did not resist as the security officers secured her hands behind her with plastic cuffs. She met Coffer's eyes as the executive officer advanced toward her slowly. "I didn't mean to hurt him," she said, her voice cold, distant. "I didn't know that I could. But it's all one now. It's too late—Div is beyond your reach, and I can't say that I'm sorry for what I did."

"Who put you up to it, Mora? Div? The *Woodman* itself?" Coffer felt her face wrinkle with sadness. "I'm afraid that for now I've no choice in what I do, Mora. Do you understand that?" Her shoulders sagged slightly. Perhaps it would have been better if the Talent had *killed* Darsen. It would all be one . . . the future for Mora would be equally bleak in either case.

For now, they would simply detain the Talent under guard in her quarters. These little cabins of the *Pegasus* could change into jails so easily. . . . Perhaps they were jail cells all the time, really.

But what was happening with *Tin Woodman?* With Mora Elbrun seen to, that was the prime question.

"Mora—do you know why Harlthor disobeyed the captain and has done this thing?"

"No," said Mora. "I only know that it was the right thing."

Coffer was inclined to agree. What to do now, though . . . send another spider ship out? Wait? Command was infinitely harder with so many options present.

Lieutenant Genson at the sensor board solved that problem rapidly with an announcement.

"Commander! *Tin Woodman* is breaking orbit!"

Coffer hesitated for a part of a second before realizing that the report had been addressed to her. She nodded curtly. "Carry on, Genson. At this point there is little we can—"

"It's on a collision course with us!"

In the vu-tank, the image of *Tin Woodman* had begun to grow rapidly. "Take evasive measures!" Coffer ordered, knowing even as she said it that the order was senseless. The *Pegasus* was too far within this system's gravitational field to use its Null-R drive, and at least a minute was needed to prepare the other engines. The starship could not take evasive action swiftly enough in normal space to avoid destruction. . . .

And the alien bore down relentlessly upon the vessel, speed constantly increasing—then simply disappeared at the last possible instant.

Something electric passed through Coffer. She leaned on the command desk to support herself. It was as though an angel's wing had brushed her—she had felt a feathery touch of the numinous—emotions beyond previous experience. It was beyond words—and Coffer could not re-create even a shadow of the sensation from memory. It was there in the instant that the *Tin Woodman* had faded incredibly from view—and now it was gone. She felt, in her soul, a deep hunger for its return.

Her gaze swept the bridge. The crew appeared similarly shaken—awe-struck, disoriented, frozen in their position as though by a spray of fairy dust. And Mora Elbrun . . .

Mora stood there between the security officers, transfixed, her mouth slack—and her eyes seemed to glimmer and sparkle briefly as though they were glass eyepieces focused into a bright and mysterious moment within her. She spoke. "Div!" As though it were the secret name of God himself.

"—just gone." Norlan from the communications console. "What?" he asked, vocalizing the question that was heavy in them all. His voice seemed to rise up from a great murk . . . a great distance.

Coffer went to Mora. "What *happened*, Mora? What *was* that?"

Mora began to smile. "He's safe now . . . safe from all of you." Her vision seemed to lose its glaze as she stared at Coffer. "You can't hurt him now."

"But what happened? Is the alien coming back? You seem to have *seen* something . . . with your Talent, Mora?"

But the woman only smiled a secret smile, and Coffer knew that they would get no explanation. Not now, at least. Christ, what a mess of things—the alien had slipped away, and they had *nothing* to show for the weeks they had loitered here, ignoring the duties of their interstellar run. The authorities would be furious.

Then suddenly Mora seemed to be loosed from her daze . . . and she tried to speak. "I saw . . ." she repeated several times, but did not seem to be able to form words to describe *what* she saw, despite Coffer's encouragement.

Finally, Coffer gave up. There were other things to be attended to. She said, "Take her down to her cabin, as previously ordered. Have Dr. Kervatz give her a mild sedative. Darsen will no doubt want her rested when he decides what he wants done with her."

PART TWO:

THE MACHINES

Whatever it was went haywire in the mechanism,
they've just about got it fixed again. The
clean, calculated arcade movement is coming
back: six-thirty out of bed, seven into the
mess hall, eight the puzzles come out for the
Chronics and the cards for the Acutes . . . in the
Nurse's station I can see the white hands of
the Big Nurse float over the controls.

—Ken Kesey

ONE FLEW OVER THE CUCKOO'S NEST

FIVE

Leana Coffer's Journal
(Vocoder transcription)

It's been rough lately—frayed nerves all over, especially mine. We've got to stay in this sector of space until we get new orders. There will doubtlessly be a long inquiry into this *Tin Woodman* affair when we reach a Triunion base—but that certainty seems almost preferable to the limbo we find ourselves in now.

Darsen's recovering quite well—so well that he gave me his first order today. Thank God he's not totally well yet; I'll be acting captain for a few days more, and the crew can rest awhile.

I visited Darsen after a tedious duty shift today. He seemed to be resting comfortably. He's still a little weak, but as ever sees himself as the Caesar of this ship, Bellerophon to this *Pegasus*.

He's ordered that Mora Elbrun be turned over to the MedSec surgeons. He wants her Doped.

No one aboard ever suspected that Mora had the power to attack Darsen the way she did. I'm still not sure she does—perhaps the alien had something to do with that. But having harmed Darsen, she's given that maniac the excuse to do what he's always wanted to do. In this instance his orders, though given for vicious personal reasons, are backed up by regulations. Were I the permanent commander of the *Pegasus*, I could bend the rules; they leave room for personal judgment. But if I defy Darsen's orders now I'll be called to account for it when he reassumes full command of the ship.

I told him about what appeared to be happening to Mora just before *Tin Woodman* vanished. That it seemed as though there was some sort of communication between them, so strong that the members of the bridge crew felt it too. I suggested that Mora is our best witness to this phenomenon, and that if we Dope her we'll lose it. But in his fury, Darsen isn't at all concerned with the negative consequences of blanking Mora. He wants his revenge.

So in my own self-interest and for the welfare of everyone who serves under Darsen, I have to allow the treatments to begin. Hopefully, my strongly worded advisory to the Triunion Council will stop them before it's too late for Mora. For the good of everyone. . . . That's really an unworthy excuse. It's *my* career that I want to protect. I'm ashamed of myself, but it takes more than moral courage to commit suicide—it takes a little craziness too. I'm too sane. So I just work out my feelings talking into this little mike— Down with Caesar! Death to the captain! How easy to say . . . how hard to even try to oppose the imperious bastard.

Death to . . . God!—I'd better put this recorder on voice-lock from now on, or be more careful what I say.

Her wheat-colored hair was reaped, and the useless harvest placed in a disposal unit.

They hadn't bothered to put her out, and she watched the cold and glistening ceremony that would end in her oblivion with detachment. Her head was clamped to an operating table. Her open eyes gazed up, fixed on the face of the surgeon who hovered, Charon-like, surveying the tool-oars about him with which he would row her across the Styx. Two nurses, gloved hands poised, flanked him. An anesthesiologist sat by her side, his attention devoted to a bank of meters which monitored her pain levels and vital signs. A painless death-that-was-not-death would be hers.

The murmur of voices, the whirs and hums of the omnipresent machinery, the antiseptic lack of scents; all were familiar to Mora, and yet simultaneously unreal. It seemed so far away, so unimportant. She'd given them no struggle. Paralyzed by a swift injection, swiftly wheeled into this MedSec operating cubicle, head shaved, connected to these padded clamps, electrodes affixed to her flesh; all of it had been a slow, soft blur lacking significance.

They were turning her over to the machines, but it didn't matter because she'd been caught up in the cogs and gears all her life, and this was the logical end.

No. It didn't matter at all.

"Bring up the sterile field," Wald Kervatz directed Nurse Vandez. She obliged with a delicate twist of a dial, which resulted in a blue nimbus of radiation suffusing the cubicle walls. A brain injection was not a complex operation, but regulations classified it as major surgery. Observation by a full surgical team was therefore required.

I could turn this over to any of them, Kervatz thought. *Let someone else watch the machines do their work.*

A surgical laser moved into place next to the subject. "First, an in-
cision will be made in the left parietal bone, just above the temporal
suture," Kervatz explained, his voice pedantic, trying to separate himself as much as possible from what was really happening. Trying not
to feel as though his hand were on the lever of a guillotine . . .

He activated the laser, and it drilled into Mora Elbrun's head. Va-
porized flesh and bone condensed quickly into carbon dust, glowing
red in the path of the laser's light. Kervatz looked up at the acoustical hologram suspended over the operating table. Floating there
was an image in carnival colors, segmented in three dimensions by a
graph marked with numbered co-ordinates, of the patient's brain.

The laser drew back, was replaced by a machine which held a hair-
fine needle. "The point of injection is controlled down to the micro-
millimeter," Kervatz said. "Psychemicidian is released only into the
angular gyrus." He turned to the anesthesiologist. "Scandon, where
did you study medicine?"

"New York Medical College," the young man replied.

Kervatz nodded. He thought he'd seen that on the lad's readout.
The doctor had studied there himself, some twenty years before.

"Was Chips still there?"

"Yes, sir. Used him in surgical training. We did have newer
models—"

"Watch the dials, Scandon." Chips had been a perfect patient; it
was a prosthesis. Chips bled, reacted to pain, vomited. Kervatz remembered the first time he'd seen Chips die. It had been in the
midst of an arterial implant Kervatz had been performing. He was
given a failing mark, the technicians cranked old Chips back up
again, and the next student had taken his turn. There'd been no
guilt, then; only the humiliation of failing a test. "This is a human
being, Scandon."

"Of course, sir."

As if that mattered, he thought. They were all machines to one another on this ship, in this universe; fleshy constructs of society. Sometimes Kervatz fancied he saw the thin little wires running out of people's heads, out of his own cranium: metallic puppet strings. *A little
tug, and watch us dance. Watch us destroy the mind of someone
who refused to dance. Watch a more substantial bit of metal drive
downward into the rebel's soul* . . .

The moment: a click, a hiss. On the holograph, a snail-slow black line moved inward, downward, penetrating the cerebral cortex: the needle.

I'm sorry, Mora. The wires are too strong.

"On target," Vandez said.

Reality twisted about her, pretzeling into moebus strips of moments that turned inside out, revolved her about. She seemed to be gazing down on it all from a spot on the ceiling, and then inconstant reality did a double flip and she was back on the table, growing fuzzy at the edges. Her body dissolved into a little cloud that began to dissipate into the sterile, odorless air, sucked up by intake ducts, cleansed from the starship's systems, ejected into space like so much worthless flotsam.

The stars, the stars—how dull, lusterless they were—marbles on the black pavement of the sky to scoot about, click into foolish games of the circular logic of a child . . . child . . . child . . .

The stars melted, congealed into the image of Kervatz's face, wet with perspiration that should not exist in the temp-controlled operating theater. It loomed before her, gigantic, close to hers. His body trailed out behind him to a tiny point—a place far away, a place she wished she were. A place of cool luster, sun-dappled snow . . .

. . . *trees stark green against glittering white. A fairy dream, pixie-dancing its pleasant cold that didn't hurt against her heart as she peered down from the safe, warm skimmer, her friend driving.*

Karen's voice broke the sweet crystalline silence. "*Tell me about your father, Mora.*"

Father. So long ago. On Earth, so strange. His face was like father's wrapped up in hospital walls. *Mora. Mora. I'm so sorry.*

Father, hospital, all white like silent snow . . .

. . . *the room was bone-white. Gauzy curtains about a window framed a piece of outside: gray sky, roofs of other buildings, an occasional aircraft cutting through the smog. Mother holding her hand. Clammy, her hand . . . uncomfortable, like all of her felt now. On a high bed with a plastic cover was Father, much too high to see. But she saw the machines. The wires and the tubes. The things running into the sickly green sheets lumped up on the bed. Father was there, yes . . . she felt him there.*

Not good . . . sick . . . ill . . . not good. The pain . . . it scared her like nothing she had ever felt before . . . not like Mother being angry, or falling down, clump. It was a pain that went places so deep, so scary; that fell into holes without bottoms.

". . . I understand . . ." The doctor speaking to Mother, who looked so desolate. "We should go into the lounge. A shame you didn't have enough insurance . . ."

Mother pulled her behind, clutching her hand hard, walking too fast. Don't be sad, Mother. Don't hurt. I hurt too when you hurt.

"I understand," the doctor continued, when they were in another room. "The financial burden—keeping him that way."

Mother lit a cigarette, which made Mora feel better; it was a part of Mother—better than the hospital smell. "You'd think with all advancements medical science has made—" *Mother said in a choking voice.*

"It was a terrible accident," said the doctor. "No one could have been prepared . . ."

"Death is like life, isn't it?" *Mother said.* "Nobody is ever prepared for either."

"We'll let you know," the doctor said. "Again, I'm sorry."

It was all so confusing. She was frightened. Inside, she ached.

The doctor stood, left. It was like he had never been there.

"Mom," *she said plaintively.* "C'mon. Let's go home. I don't like to be here. I don't like to be around Dad this way. Can we take him home?"

And Mother grabbed her arm so hard, shook her till her teeth rattled. Her face was like a monster's. "Don't you understand, you little shit? You'll never see Dad again! Never! Can't you feel that with your goddamned Talent your goddamned father insisted we keep? Damn you, Mora." *Her teeth were clenched; tears were running out of her eyes.* "If you weren't here, maybe I'd have the money. But oh no. He wanted a little girl, no matter what the cost is these days. And he didn't know it, but it cost him his life. Damn you to hell!"

At first all she felt was numb shock. And then the pain began, fiercer than she'd ever felt before, even worse than when they took her to the special doctors to have her tested. It slipped into her mind like a hot knife: her flash of hatred, barbed with her words. Never see Dad again? Never? Never? And Mother seemed so very distant, running away . . . leaving her alone . . . separated . . . so all alone.

Mother let go, and she found herself falling onto the carpeted floor—falling and screaming, it hurt so much.

Suddenly, her mother was pulling her up again, clutching her hard, and she felt waves of sorrow and self-hate from her. "I'm sorry, baby. Oh, God, Mora, I didn't mean it, darling. Forgive me."

Other people were around them now, their alien feelings crowding her, making her feel closed in. She threw her little arms around Mother's neck, and sheltered herself in familiarity . . . but Mother seemed so strange now, so distant.

She didn't understand . . . she didn't understand at all.

A finger. The tip of a finger grew before her eye. The finger was holding up an eyelid, and it moved away enough for her to see the vague shapes of ghostly people-things before her.

"She's fighting it," said a voice.

An angry voice responded, "Well, what do you expect?"

It was all so white. So very white. She felt the pressure of the finger ease and her eyelid slid slowly back.

But it was still so white . . . so very white . . .

"He died when I was four," she says, looking at the silver-white snow as it slides by beneath the skimmer. "I don't want to talk about it now."

"Sure," Karen says. "Fathers usually mess up a girl's mind, in some way. I understand. How about your mother?"

"Right now, she's on a colony. A planet circling Fomalhaut. She went there when I was six. I've not seen her since. She sent money and letters."

"Around Fomalhaut? What's the name of that planet—can't remember. I've heard about it. Warm. Always warm. Not like here—right now it's anything but warm."

"I like the winter," she responds. "It's so peaceful."

"And are your thoughts peaceful?" Karen asks.

Mora turns around in the passenger seat of the skimmer, looks at her friend steering wildly over the drifts, like waves on a white sea. "You don't know?"

"Wasn't sure you wanted me in your head, just now. You look so somber. Oh hell, that damned wind." She takes her hands away from the controls, catches at her long red hair. "Hey—hand me my hat." It is tucked down below the seats. Mora hands it to her, and Karen pulls it down over her ears, pushing her hair up under it.

I wish she wouldn't be so reckless, Mora thinks.

And you worry too much, you know? Relax. Karen thought-casts. Enjoy the scenery.

The landscape is beautiful. Though the skimmer isn't enclosed and the heating stasis-bubble isn't working well, and the wind at eighty-nine kays an hour is fierce, it is worth it. The pale blue crystal dome of the sky in these mountains is like no place else Mora has ever been. Karen is keeping the skimmer down low, almost grazing the tops of trees. Some are tall white cones, their branches alive with foliage laden with ice and snow. Others stand stark, gray, solitary— like sentinels guarding some precious unknown. Looking behind them, she sees the path of the skimmer—how the white powder has been whipped into whirlwinds by their passage.

Karen reaches under the seat and pulls out a flask. She unseals it, takes a drink. She makes a face and hands the container to Mora, who swallows a gulp of the stuff with effort. "Worst whiskey in the world," *she comments.* "Has to be."

"Yeah," *Karen agrees, steering the skimmer suddenly into a great leftward arc, heading off toward the frozen lake.* "Rig's stuff. He's really not very good at it, yet. Keeps trying."

"I think he's carrying self-sufficiency too far," *Mora says.* "Better just to go into town."

"I think Rig would have a seizure if he had to deal with a Normal," *Karen says, laughing.* "I really do." *The thought strikes both of them as tremendously funny and Mora doesn't stop laughing until Karen nearly runs the skimmer into the roof of a cabin near the lake.* "Geez. Better take her up a hundred meters or so," *Karen says.*

"Better not get any drunker," *Mora says.* "You'll kill us both."

"Sometimes I don't believe you're real, Mora. How did you get to be such a worry-wart in fifteen years?"

"I've had a lot to worry about." *Suddenly, Mora feels the need to communicate the calm, the joy that she has experienced here so far away from Normals. . . .*

A roar splits the air, shaking the skimmer. Karen leans forward, intent on her manipulation of the craft's controls. Mora looks up. There, above, is the red glow of a shuttle craft, speeding across the sky. The thunder dies away.

"Damn thing," *Karen says, finally regaining control of the skimmer and looking up with Mora.* "We caught its shock wave."

"It's a cargo shuttle," *Mora comments.* "Only things big enough to generate a shock wave like that. Probably resupplying the Orion, which is in Earth-orbit right now, expecting a—"

Karen interrupts. "You certainly know enough about those things."

"*My father was a shuttle pilot. I don't really remember him, of course, but I got interested when I was at school . . .*" She lets the sentence trail off, falling into thought. "*You know, the Philadelphia Starport is just a few kilometers away. The rest of the world is just beyond those mountains—it seems so far away . . .*"

"*This is the world,*" Karen insists. "*What's out there . . . well, the Normals made it. Let them live in it.*"

A sudden fear grips her. A fleeting foreshadow of loss . . . ? "*And if they decide they don't like us here, grouped like we are?*"

Karen doesn't answer. Mora looks out at the horizon. Darkness is falling so suddenly . . . it isn't really that late, and yet it is becoming harder and harder to make out anything. "*I won't let them blank me. I want to live,*" Mora says suddenly, not understanding why. She turns to Karen.

Karen is gone. The skimmer is gone.

"*It's finally taking effect, Doctor.*"

Finally . . . finally . . . finally . . . final . . . fin . . .

Darkness comes. It congeals into a light-veined gel which seems to suck her down, smothering her. With a vivid flash, she remembers everything. But the darkness relentlessly drags her down toward a yawning chasm. "*Damn you all!*" she screams with her mind. "*I want to live!*"

It is a revelation.

But the darkness is deaf as death itself.

Ston didn't think it was too serious an injury. But his left hand hurt, and by the time he reached MedSec it was swollen.

He and Bif Hersil, another newly commissioned ensign in the engineering section, had been doing some maintenance work. They'd been lifting a heavy piece of metal shielding into an airlock, preparing to go EVA and repair a portion of the outer hull which had sustained minor meteorite damage.

"Pretty brainy work, this," Hersil had griped amiably, his teeth clenched with the effort of hoisting the plate. "For this I learned hyperspacial field mechanics?"

Ston had been holding the metal plate by its other end. "A hallowed tradition—hard work initiation of the green officers." But unlike most "traditions" of the Triunion Space Service, this one ostensibly had a purpose. The greatest danger aboard a starship as huge as this was that the crew would start thinking of it as a self-sustaining world. Let them do a little machine-work, reasoned the brass: maintain the hull, clean the air-filtration and waste-circulation units; then they won't forget so easily where they are. "You got a good grip?" Bif had nodded. "Let's move it, then."

As Ston had begun to back into the airlock, however, he was distracted. For just a moment he thought—he was *sure*—that someone had called out to him. Not Bif—no, it had sounded like . . . it had sounded like Adria, his sister.

Which was impossible, because Adria was dead.

In that disoriented moment the metal plate had slipped through the fingers of his right hand, falling hard against the frame of the airlock door and pinching his left hand beneath it for just a moment before crashing to the floor.

So now Ston was sitting slouched in a MedSec waiting room chair, in full pressure suit minus gloves. The duty nurse looked up from paperwork, squinting hawkish young features at him when a small plastic mound on his desk blinked pink. "Ah—someone'll be with you in a minute. Don't let them amputate. We've only got right hands in stock for grafting purposes." Ston knew him casually. Ven something or other. Ven showed perfect white teeth in a smile.

Everybody in the service seems to have teeth like that, thought Ston. Well, dental implants were a part of the Service Health Coverage Plan. Ston still had his originals, but he was seriously considering new ones. Maybe it was good for them all to have perfect teeth and broad shoulders here on the good ship *Pegasus*. They were all heroes, weren't they? On Earth, Crysor, and Deva, anyway.

Pain, Ston decided, was making him unaccustomedly cynical. Yet it was true: explorers of new lands, discoverers of new riches, bringers of knowledge, the human beings who crewed the starships were indeed heroes on the home worlds. The starships themselves, creations of the vast pooled technologies of three worlds, had become uncomfortably like objects of worship themselves.

So what did that make him? he wondered. A high priest of the Order of the Cog? Lugging steel plating around, yet.

"You all right?" Ven asked.

Ston realized he'd been ignoring the nurse. "My hand just hurts," he mumbled. "If you don't hurry this process up, I'm going to bleed on your desk."

"Hey—don't blame me," Ven protested. "I'm just—" A door at the end of the waiting room slid open and a middle-aged, dark-haired man in a MedSec uniform entered. He stopped at the duty nurse's desk to have a word with him. Ston couldn't hear most of what he said, but he picked up the name "Mora Elbrun."

The temptation to walk over and join the conversation was strong, but Ston resisted it. He knew about as much concerning Captain Darsen's injury two days ago as most of the crew, which was very little. Those members of the bridge crew who had witnessed it had been ordered to keep tight teeth on the subject. It had been rumored that *Tin Woodman* had somehow caused the incident before it vanished. And that Mora Elbrun had been involved. Ston remembered talking to her, less than an hour before she'd . . . done whatever she'd done. Try as he might, he couldn't imagine how she—

"You waiting to see a doctor, son?" The man at Ven's desk had turned toward him, was addressing him.

"Yes, sir." Ston rose and moved to him, extending his bandaged hand. "Bit of an accident."

"Let me see that." The man carefully unwound the rag which Ston had wrapped around his left hand. "I'm chief surgeon. Dr. Kervatz. Don't believe I've met you."

"Ensign Ston Maurtan, sir," he responded, watching apprehensively as Kervatz took the hand by its fingers. Experimentally, the doctor grasped the thumb with his other hand, moved it, just a bit. Pain shot through Ston's hand; he couldn't help the ragged intake of breath, the low moan.

"Hurt?" Kervatz inquired, half-smiling.

"I guess you could say that, sir," he replied, testily.

"It should. You've had an accident. We fragile machines can't afford being careless. Pain is our body's warning system—and it's a kind of penance too, I think."

"Sort of a cruel way of seeing it, sir," Ston interrupted, his hand still throbbing. Realizing he was out of line, he tried to backpedal— "I mean—"

"No, no," Kervatz said, nodding absently, preoccupied with something else entirely it seemed. "It certainly doesn't behoove me, that particular philosophy. . . . Well, in any case, young man, my expert guess is that you've fractured your phalanx."

"Sir?"

"Most likely a hairline fracture in one of the bones of your thumb. Nothing serious, but smarts like the devil, I dare say. Go down to 4-B, have a nurse scanner it to confirm my hypothesis. She'll set it, if that's what you need. And have yourself relieved from active duty for forty-eight hours. My orders."

"Thank you, sir." He flashed a sincere smile. Forty-eight hours was generous. Backing away, a bit overwhelmed by being attended to by the chief surgeon himself, he didn't notice the young MedSec doctor coming through the door. There was a glancing collision; Ston turned to apologize, but the man didn't seem to care at all, his attention directed entirely on Kervatz.

"Elbrun is in 4-A," the young doctor said, "resting well. She's strong. We'll be able to proceed with the second injection on schedule."

Ston stopped, listened. They didn't even seem to notice his presence.

Kervatz frowned. "You seem pretty eager, Scandon. You'll be pleased to know that I've turned the matter over to you."

"Me, sir?"

"That's right. You need the experience. Not that anything's involved. The first injection did most of the preliminary damage, although it won't take if she doesn't get another in twenty-four hours. You'll notice that she'll begin to show normal responses to her surroundings before that time, though most likely they'll be feeble. Like you said, she's strong. She'll fight. I'll double-check you from time to time, of course."

Ston noted the pleasure Scandon was taking in all this. It made him feel ill. Before they noticed he was listening, he turned into the corridor, walked a few steps until he heard the door slide shut behind him. He stopped and tried to collect his thoughts.

Injections? Mora Elbrun was a Talent—like Adria. And she'd done something . . . harmed Darsen? If so, she'd be Doped—Adria had told him all about that. There were very strict regulations about Talents.

He had to find out.

A nurse breezed out from a room a few doors down, strode efficiently ahead of him, not looking back. The door to that room had been left open. Ston stepped inside. There was a woman in the room, lying on a form-couch. Mora Elbrun.

Standing beside her, Ston touched her forehead lightly with his good hand. She seemed to be sleeping. Her hair was gone. "Mora? Mora, it's Ston Maurtan." His hand moved to her bare shoulder, shook it. Her eyelids slowly lifted. The pupils were dilated, making her coral eyes larger than ever. She opened her mouth, but didn't speak. No, not asleep. Drugged. There was a cast to her eyes, as if she was light-years away . . . it was like peering into two bottomless, empty wells.

"Mora," Ston whispered, an insane idea dawning on him. "Mora, did you call me?" No response. There was nothing he could do right now, he realized.

Approaching footsteps echoed down the outside corridor. He dashed back out, just before the nurse he'd seen depart before turned the corner, carrying a tray of medical supplies. Ston let her walk down to him. "I'm lost," he said, averting his face sheepishly. "Could you tell me where 4-B is?"

"Go back to the main corridor and make a right," the woman answered brusquely, stepping past him, and into Mora's room. She closed the door behind her. Ston noted the usual simple electronic lock of the sort crew quarters were outfitted with.

That was good.

"I may be crazy, Mora Elbrun," he mumbled to himself, walking toward the MedSec room to be mended. "But I can't let them do this to you."

SIX

Leana Coffer's Journal
(Vocoder transcription authorized
by Leana Coffer. Original recording
voice-locked per program 774-D.)

Acting captain—Ha! What a joke. One of the first things that Darsen did upon reassuming command was to order his flunky, Jin Tamner, to prepare and have sent by Norlan a formal report of what transpired during the attempt at contact with *Tin Woodman*. It "superseded" the report I prepared; mine wasn't even transmitted.

Dr. Kervatz sent me a report on the first of Mora's treatments. She's going under fast. Maybe two more treatments, and they'll make an ideal citizen of her. Of course, someone will have to feed her; she won't be able to do those things any more.

To think that at one time I was idealistic about the service, back at the academy. Such a feeling of commitment—I worked so hard for my commission. I remember feeling that I'd blown it, the time that I got into a political demonstration and got arrested by the MP's . . . then when the commission came through anyway, how overjoyed I was.

So here I am at thirty-six, believing in nothing, looking off into some terrible future which I feel Darsen is planning. If I had something to believe in, I'd give my life to it. I don't even believe in myself.

I envy Mora. What motivated her to sacrifice herself for a stranger? Because he was a Talent? That alone seems an unlikely explanation. If only I could talk to her, find out.

And what of Div? He gave himself as well, in a way. What has happened to him and the alien that swallowed him up? I'll never know, I guess—and yet there's nothing in the universe I'd rather know, if that experience on the bridge was a taste of it . . .

Far away, the memory replayed itself for the being who had been called Div Harlthor. Again he saw it all, and it took on new meaning, scintillating light into new crevices of revelation:

The swim through space, sensing the void-spider behind him, weaving its invisible web of deadly intent down toward him. Hurry, must hurry, or all is lost. And always there is a beacon-like transmission, pulling him, tugging him to what must be where Tin Woodman *wanted him. . . . The soft impact with the hull, the feeling of it tingling through the palms of his pressure suit gloves. And yet, no access door! Panic. And, simultaneously, a soothing feeling of well-being. All is well, it says, and it is not from within him. Suddenly, the parting of the hull. Quickly, he slips in. Into the darkness. He turns and the opening slowly seals away the stars and the fruitlessly clutching spider ship of Edan Darsen. The darkness is total, and yet not at all frightening. A comfortable, life-giving darkness. He becomes aware of a hissing sound—air? Yes, this must be some sort of airlock. The hissing stops, and the lip of darkness parts into the interior of the ship. He steps out into it and into awe.*

Trusting, he removes his pressure suit. He is standing in a long, winding corridor of some resilient pink substance. Its texture is smooth; warm to the touch. Like a womb, he thinks. A mad, Freudian fantasy. He shakes the idea off. The air is sweet and moist and warm.

Out of the depths of the dimly luminescent passage ahead of him the mind of the ship-being reaches out . . .

FOLLOW.

Alien thoughts lead him through the labyrinth, slowly, toward the creature's center. It seems as though he travels far through this round tunnel, so suffused with rose light. Off every twist, every surface, the ship's consciousness reverberates one great empty emotion, echoing until the air seems to roar with it.

ALONENESS. DRIFTING WITHOUT PURPOSE AMONG THE STARS . . . THE BURNING FIRES TOUCHING VUL . . . DEATH, PAIN . . . HOLLOW LONELINESS.

Something builds within him. Somehow, he senses movement of the ship . . . he feels contact with this ship-being more and more . . . flooding in . . . lovely, beautiful . . .

He staggers, falls into spongy tissue with exquisite pleasure . . . and abruptly is aware that he is more than just himself—his senses extend much further. He reaches out to a tender spark in the void before him . . . and finds that it is Mora Elbrun . . . in an instant, he sees what she has done for him, and knows why . . . for a moment, he stands on the bridge of the starship Pegasus, *looking and feeling all of it through Mord's senses.*

It is all right, *he finds himself telling her.* See through me as well. See what is happening to me. *And he could feel her experience his change as well, as her being briefly once more merged with his as it had in her cabin—and he showed her the things he was experiencing . . .*

Then the abrupt breakage of contact—the slithery slide into a different dimension of space—the fear . . . and the comfort.

ALL IS WELL. I HAVE POWER ONCE MORE. WE ARE LEAVING QUICKLY.

He starts to question this but realizes that there will be plenty of time for questions. So much to learn. He rises back to his feet and proceeds into the heart of the ship-being.

It was part of his Learning and Acclimatization, this constant reanalysis of the content and substances of the first meeting. It is the Rosetta stone of meaning for his new comprehension. TAKE IT BACK TO THE ENTRY INTO THE CORRIDOR, said the ship-being. WHAT IS A "WOMB"?

Ston Maurtan was proud of his service record.

After a top 10 per cent showing in his academy class on Crysor, his Voyage Training accomplishments had been so exemplary, he received his commission and ship assignment after merely eight months aboard the *Valkyrie*. While on this training cruiser, he'd been granted a week's leave of absence so that he might attend the funeral of his sister, Adria, on Earth. His return was two hours beyond the time designated on his ship's LOA document. This had been the only infraction of regulations logged against him since he'd stuffed his DI's boots with mashed potatoes in his first year at the academy.

The only other infraction he'd been caught at, anyway.

An intercom just above blared, startling him: "Attention. All officers on Bridge Crew 'A' will please report to briefing lounge 3-C immediately. . . . Attention. All officers on Bridge Crew—"

Damn. What was wrong with his nerves? He'd always imagined that in stress situations he'd be cool, but now he found himself battling a surprising amount of simple, uncomplicated fear. He tuned out the sudden intrusion of noise upon his concentrated effort to beat back that fear. Control yourself, man, he told himself. For in the last twelve hours Ensign Ston Maurtan had committed two court-martial offenses. At the moment he was contemplating the third. Self-control was everything, now.

Uncertainty, not guilt, caused his blood to race, his hands to tremble slightly at unexpected sounds. Quite suddenly, he felt cut off from the others aboard the *Pegasus*. He had no allies in this, no friends in whom he might confide these necessary things he'd done to save Mora.

Court-martial offenses. The past hours raced over and over in his head:

Following Dr. Kervatz's orders, he had gone directly from treatment in MedSec to the Engineering Office to report the necessary forty-eight-hour absence from duty his injury had caused. Lingering there, he visited the electronics shop, where he illicitly pocketed certain items of hardware, failing to have their nature recorded or their price debited to his ship's account. Back in his quarters, he waited for his roommate's necessary duty-shift departure, then constructed a simple device capable of blocking electronic signals to magnetic locks.

After locating Mora's quarters in the ship's directory, he used his new lock pick to enter the compartment. There he found her MedSec uniform. It fit him poorly—blouse too narrow across shoulders and chest; pants too long in leg; baggy about the rear section. But it was identical to all the other MedSec uniforms, and would have to serve as the needed camouflage to mask his intended activities.

A brisk walk and lift-chute jump later, he was striding outside the MedSec offices. There was no one in sight. His luck was holding up. He selected the correct door, clamped his device to the wall, tapped its button. The door whispered open obediently and Ston walked through, mindful of the directory schematic he'd memorized. He was in the post-operative recovery cell, which adjoined Mora's recuperation chamber, connected by another door. He applied his lock pick to that door.

The chamber that was revealed to him by the door's opening was dim, lit solely by a small lamp near the medical form-couch upon which Mora lay unconscious. She was not alone. A nurse was leaning over her.

"What are you doing here?" Ston challenged immediately, blurting the first thing that flashed into his mind. He shifted the lock-pick mechanism to his injured left hand.

"Huh?" The man straightened up hesitantly, turned around. A big man, he almost eclipsed the lamplight. "Why, uh, Vandez put this on my rounds. I'm to administer—"

Drawing in a breath, Ston stepped forward, delivered a hard blow to the nurse's chin with his good hand. The fist shut the nurse up, but hardly fazed him more than that. Ston desperately rabbit-punched him again, gave him a few clumsy karate chops, which managed to bring him to his knees. He kneed him in the jaw, brought the lock pick down on the back of his head as a last resort. The plastic case smashed, scattering the jerry-rigged circuitry components on the floor.

The nurse grunted and banged onto the floor, unconscious.

Fiery pain coursed up Ston's left arm from the blow's impact. He clenched his teeth, choked back a scream.

Once more in control, he paced over to the form-couch's control panel. "Mora—can you hear me?" he whispered harshly. When there was no response, he activated the couch's motor. Its low hum seemed to his jangled nerves a huge roar. Mora stirred, her head lolling from side to side on the pillow. But she didn't speak. Her eyes, half-opened, seemed unable to focus. He knew she couldn't understand him, but he spoke nevertheless: "It's going to be all right."

As he looked down on her, for a moment he seemed to be gazing at Adria.

Shrugging off the illusion, he found the lever that disengaged the couch from its wall-and-motor attachment. The bed rolled away slightly on its four wheels. He pushed it past the snoring man on the floor into the post-op room. After poking his head out the main door, he steered the bed into the still-empty corridor, wheeled it toward the lift chute.

He'd just arrived when a lift platform sighed down. On it was a tall man wearing the maroon and gold of command crew. Ston didn't know him; he checked the ID badge over the left breast pocket. Lieutenant Norlan. Ston gulped silently, flashed a small smile, praying the expression would hold Norlan's gaze so that the man wouldn't pay undue attention to the medical couch's passenger.

Norlan returned the smile. "Going up?"

"Down." Ston shook his head. "I mean, I'll wait for the next lift."

Norlan nodded absently, punched a control. The lift rose.

Ston felt perspiration bead on his brow, dampen his palms.

When the lift returned empty, he guided the couch into it, dialed out the special sleeper deck code on the controls. The lift eased down, not helping the queasiness he felt in his abdomen.

To take his mind off his fear and sickness, he considered the sleeper deck.

The environmental systems of the *Pegasus* were capable of sustaining approximately a thousand persons, although the ship's crew numbered half that many. But a starship cruiser of this sort performed many functions. Right now, aboard the *Pegasus*, close to a hundred civilian scientists engaged in deep-space research. Then there were the crews of ten small stellar exploration spacecraft the *Pegasus* was ferrying to a number of distant star systems. Four hundred and twenty-one military individuals and technicians bound for existing colonies near the edge of Triunion space were on board, as well as colonists being transported to newly chartered settlements along the *Pegasus'* intended route.

To accomplish the hauling of these people, an entire section of the *Pegasus* was outfitted with two thousand Henderson capsules—black, sarcophagus-like cryogenic units, each able to hold one person in suspended animation for years. All of the *Pegasus'* human supercargo, including the nine hundred and eighty-four prospective colonists bound for two new worlds, were presently sealed in the starship's Hendersons.

This was sleeper deck.

The platform halted. Before Ston were the cold corridors of his destination. There were no duty stations on this deck. The ship's computer monitored the conditions of the Hendersons, which were efficiently racked in long, monotonous, uniform rows. Ston guided Mora's couch between the close rows of these black metal boxes, relaxing. This part was planned very carefully; it should run smoothly.

He eased up to the first available empty capsule, opened it, lifted Mora in, hooking up the waste evacuation and breathing equipment. He did not activate the cryogenic circuits; should Mora recover from her single psychemicidian injection, her metabolism would have to remain normal. Therefore, to prevent the monitor computer from sounding an alarm because of the unit's "malfunctioning" freezer device, he'd have to cut the sensor cable before he initiated power into—

Damn. He'd forgotten the wire cutters.

Praying that it would be enough, he yanked at the sensor cable with his good hand. The cable held a moment . . . then jerked free.

Relieved, he set it down on the floor in a space he hoped no one would notice. Then he pulled down the lid of the Henderson, switched on the air supply and the emergency heating coils.

He double-checked everything to ascertain that nothing would malfunction. Reasonably satisfied, he grabbed hold of the empty med-couch and wheeled it back to wait for the lift platform.

So many offenses, each one grounds for court-martial . . .

A repeat announcement from the speakers brought him out of his reverie into the reality of the present moment. There was no use counting up the offenses now. The number dwindled into insignificance. They'd number them for him when they caught him—which they probably would. He had ditched the couch in an equipment storage area where it was not likely to be found, but as soon as Mora's disappearance was discovered and announced, it was only a matter of time before Lieutenant Norlan put two and two together and pointed his face out on the personnel roster. And had that nurse gotten a good look at his face? Probably.

He had botched it.

But there was no use stopping now. The momentum he had built up was too great. Perhaps the inertia would carry him through.

In any case, he had no regrets for what he had done. And no second thoughts about what he was going to do.

Like most of the starship's rooms of function, the briefing lounge was severely military. The transition from the comfort-oriented living and entertainment quarters was always a noticeable one to Lieutenant Gary Norlan. It was almost as though the environment itself called for attention, discipline, and restraint in one's duties. But as he settled in one of the briefing table's straight-backed, hard-plastic chairs, it was the captain who called for the immediate attention of the assembled members of Bridge Crew A.

"Where is Dr. Kervatz?" he demanded, as though one of them might be hiding the man. Captain Edan Darsen was obviously still weak, and yet his almost manic inner intensity backboned him into performing his duty, despite his ill-health. He refused to stay in bed.

It was Tamner who immediately responded. "He's not bridge crew, Captain. You only ordered—"

Darsen's eyes betrayed an uncharacteristic anxiousness—usually hard and cold, they now darted about, searching the faces of those assembled for—something. Norlan felt a queasy sensation when those eyes lighted on him. They looked out from a severely disturbed consciousness. "Kervatz's attendance here is necessary," he stated, his big bass voice louder than necessary. "What I have to say will concern him. Have him paged."

Tamner immediately rose from his seat beside the captain and left the room. Funny. Tamner had never been this close to the captain's confidence before—he must have wormed into it only recently, convincing the obviously paranoid captain that he could be trusted.

"Now then," Darsen began gruffly. "I called this meeting to inform you that I have just received orders from Galactic Command which alter the mission status of this vessel."

So that was it, thought Norlan. But why did Darsen sound so hesitant—almost unsure of himself. Something strange was going on.

Norlan glanced at the faces of his fellow officers. They all wore the same solemn, military mask as his own. No one was going to expose his feelings here. But the executive officer—Leana Coffer—had a controlled fire of rage in her eyes.

"Our new orders are available through the ship's computer log. You are to read them in full," Darsen continued. "For now, however, I want to cover the immediately relevant portions.

"In response to this ship's transmitted report concerning the _Tin Woodman_ incident and the assault upon myself it precipitated, Galactic Command has ordered the _Pegasus_ to pursue _Tin Woodman_, now regarded as a hostile alien—"

What?

"Captain?" Norlan interrupted, unable to stop himself. Darsen's busy eyebrows rose, but Norlan continued, his mask crumbling. "I am the chief communications officer aboard this ship. I would like to know _who_ authorized that report's transmission—I've never _seen_ it. Nor have I seen _any_ incoming communication from the GC."

"I authorized it, of course," Darsen replied curtly. "Jin Tamner drafted the report from my dictation from MedSec, and had the—ah —communications officer on duty at the time make the top-secret transmission to Crysor. Tamner also personally received the response. As it happened, both times you were off duty."

"Might I remind the captain that regulations require both my authorization of outgoing transmission and my cognizance of incoming—"

"_My_ prerogative, Lieutenant." Darsen's voice rose above Norlan's imperiously. "*I* am the captain of this ship! I am yet capable of performing my duties!"

Common sense and discretion dictated that Norlan accept this. But the abuse of regulations irritated him. That—and something more. "I should very much like to see a copy of this report."

Darsen glared at him. "It is secret material, classified under my own personal code," he snapped. His gaze swept the others at the table. "This ship is considered to be on combat alert from this point on, as per our orders from Galactic Command. And *my* orders are to be carried out without argument or—"

"Of course," said Norlan quietly, relinquishing his ground. "You are the captain, as you've said." He was startled by Darsen's loss of control, by his dictatorial response to what was surely a justifiable challenge to his procedure. The only explanation for it was that he was hiding something. He had falsified the report in some way—perhaps even altered the orders from Galactic Command. But why?

Darsen seemed to have calmed himself. "Our first priority must be to determine *Tin Woodman*'s intended course when it left the vicinity of this system. Genson."

Lieutenant Genson, the Chief Sensor Monitor, stood. "Captain, I'm sure you realize that this is not possible with our equipment. Begging your pardon . . ." She paused nervously. Darsen's outburst had unnerved them all.

". . . but when a ship drops into non-relative space, it doesn't leave a trail of any kind in this universe. No ionization, neutrinos from fusion exhaust—nothing. *Tin Woodman* would have had to have told us—"

"Yes." And Darsen began to smile. "This is true. I believe, though, that we still might be able to question *Tin Woodman*, after a fashion."

But that was crazy! thought Norlan.

"This is why I wish Dr. Kervatz present. Mora Elbrun might—" The briefing room door slid open just then, and Jin Tamner stalked back into the room, his expression disconcerted. Kervatz was not with him. "Well?" Darsen said, obviously impatient.

"Elbrun is gone," Tamner announced.

Darsen's expression grew blank. "What?"

"I just talked to Kervatz. She's not in her cubicle."

"Impossible," Darsen growled. "She couldn't even *move!*"

"She must have had help. A nurse was found unconscious in the room. He can't identify his attacker other than the fact the guy was wearing a MedSec uniform."

"Order a search immediately. Alert Security at once!" It was an alarmed order; a yell.

Norlan noticed however that Executive Officer Coffer wore a very small smile on her face. He decided that he would have to have a private conversation with her soon concerning this madness.

SEVEN

"Suspicion always haunts the guilty mind;
The thief doth fear each bush an officer."

Ston Maurtan had a fondness for Shakespeare; the lines from *Henry VI* flashed readily to mind now, assuming personal, ominous meaning. A guilty mind?—no, still not guilty. But in the last hours he had come to know suspicion quite well. Suspicion and fear.

Glancing over his shoulder warily, he stepped into the lift just outside his cabin door. The bundle of clothing he tightly clasped under one arm seemed dreadfully conspicuous. Surely the first security guard who got a glimpse of it would know they were intended for the fugitive esper. He was braced for the sudden hand on the shoulder, the weapon pressed against his back . . .

He focused on the deck lights as they rushed upward past the translucence of the lift-tube walls. He tried to shove his trepidation out of his head.

The search had been in progress ten hours now, and he had yet to be questioned. A good sign. Crew quarters were still being scrutinized, the work areas and storage rooms of Engineering ransacked for the merest clue. No one had checked sleeper deck yet. No doubt it was assumed that the ship's computer would alert them to abnormalities there. Most reassuring were the facts that the nurse he had clobbered evidently was unable to identify him, and that Norlan had apparently forgotten him. Or maybe he was withholding the information. If so, that was *very* good. Norlan knew Mora; perhaps Ston was not the only person on the *Pegasus* who cared about her fate.

The lift hushed to a halt. Ston stepped out on sleeper deck and strode to Mora's Henderson capsule.

Mora dreamed.
Amid the fuzzy contours that bordered this faintly blurred yet

strangely stark vision, she crawled, inching along a floor somewhere in the *Pegasus*. All the sights swirling about her were robed in semidarkness. Cries and shouts clamored. Hissing light flares suddenly illuminated the scene. There was fighting, all about her. A battle, surrealistically staged . . .

This dream had visited her before, breaking up the long darkness that shrouded her. Each time, it had startled her into a semiwakefulness, too faint to cry out, incapable of moving, in darkness. She felt entombed then. Perhaps these periods were as illusory as the nightmare conflict. But then she would plummet back into a deeper darkness.

A faint voice drew her up out of the depths: "Mora . . . Mora, can you wake up?"

It felt as though she was drifting up through a thick musty muck, toward a swath of new light. She strained . . . pushed hard, and the voice grew clearer. The dark parted grudgingly, and she was there. "Look at me, come on . . ." the voice was saying. She realized that she was looking up at someone, not entirely in focus. The hazy sight resolved into recognizable features . . . and it was Ston. Ston Maurtan, leaning over her.

"That's right. Just me. Now let's get you out of there," he urged in soft, concerned tones. Grasping her right arm carefully, he eased her up into a sitting position. She gazed about herself, disoriented. Where was she? This area was unfamiliar. Was she still on the *Pegasus*? Or was this yet another illusion dredged up from her slumbering subconscious.

Ston asked, "Can you slip down, stand up?"

Mora stared blankly at him, then nodded groggily. She pulled herself over the Henderson's lip, climbed down, stood wobbly by the side of the capsule. She staggered, nearly falling, but Ston braced her with strong hands. "Well," he said. "At least you're awake and alive. That's something."

"Ston . . . Maurtan," she murmured.

"Right ho. Nice of you to remember. Here we go." He handed her a bundle of clothing. "See if you can pull this on. Engineering uniform. They'll spot you in a moment if you're still in those MedSec Op duds."

"Who'll spot me?" Mora asked, accepting the clothing. "Why shouldn't they?" It didn't make sense on one level—and yet, it *felt* right. Obediently, she removed the plain white shift, began to don the uniform. "Where are we going?"

"Engineering first," he explained. "Listen. I busted you out of MedSec and brought you down here—the ship's cryogenic vault section. The alarm has been out on you for a while now—Coffer's got Security combing the whole boat for you. And if we don't get off soon, they'll jam that needle in your head again and *keelhaul* me."

"Coffer? Keelhaul?" The facts didn't align properly; she was confused.

"Ancient naval expression." He held her hands imploringly. "It's not important. What *is* important is that we jump the *Pegasus* soon. Understand?"

"But how? Are we still in the Aldebaran system?" She finished slipping the tunic on and sealed it.

"Yes. Still in orbit. Now, as to how we get out, I've figured that out. God knows maybe I would have turned myself in long before, but for this one chance. Div's ship—the messenger ship that brought him out here? They're going to jettison the thing—not worth the space taken up, or the mass to haul. Its last run knocked hell out of it. I happened on the report in Engineering. It's still in serviceable shape for one more journey, if we take care. Because you see, when they boost it out to become interstellar debris, we're going to be in it."

She attempted to read him, but couldn't. God, her thoughts were scrambled. Had the Dope washed out her Talent? She found herself suffused with both joy and grief at the possibility. To be Normal . . . and yet, if so, her specialness was gone. But no—only one injection, Ston had said. Not enough. Ston . . .

"Ston—are you all right?" she asked, deciding that she could trust him.

"Me? Yes, of course—"

"Never mind. I had a nightmare . . . you were involved."

He grinned. "Always great to have women dream about me." His expression grew grim. "But we'd better get on with it."

"Yes. I'll do whatever you say." Even as she spoke, the details of the dream faded, slipping from memory.

But she knew it would come again.

Bif Hersil leaned over the microphone attached to the launch monitor. "Programming complete," he intoned crisply, businesslike.

"Request permission to proceed with jettison." He peered through the thick plastic window of Hangar Deck Control at the robot cranes positioning the cylindrical Mark IV above the hangar doors.

"Acknowledged," replied the launch computer. "Proceed as directed." A quick touch to a glowing console plate before him activated the pre-programmed launch sequence.

There was a hush of air behind him—the door opening. Ston Maurtan stepped into the room.

"Moving up in the ranks, eh?" said Maurtan, smiling. He settled easily into a chair close to Hersil. "At last you're awarded a task befitting your inestimable talents."

Hersil grinned back at him. "Yep. Completing a computer circuit." He held up his forefinger, gazed at it sardonically. "This is all the computer needs. I could have left my brain up in quarters. Hey —how's the hand?"

"Itches under the bandage." Maurtan glanced at the instrument array before him. Above the air-pressure indicator, a chronometer was flashing out the minutes and seconds remaining before the hangar depressurization commenced: 4:57 it said. Then 4:56. "Got bored with staring at the video in my cabin. Thought I'd hop down here, watch you make this trash dump."

"Don't know as I'd call it trash," mused Hersil, regarding the messenger ship. "Put a little work into it, and it might be all right. But the brass doesn't want to bother."

"Only you on duty?"

"Might be somebody in the observation rooms. I doubt it though. Don't tell me that after all the time you've spent on starships these things still interest you."

"Well—actually I brought somebody down with me. You know Ensign Welbourne?"

Hersil shook his head.

"He's down there right now, matter of fact." Ston stabbed a finger toward the figure that walked across the hangar doors, toward the Mark IV.

"He's crazy," cried Hersil, jerking his attention away from Ston, as planned. "Ston, the hangar bay seals automatically at five minutes until . . ." He checked the chronometer. "He'll be killed! I'll have to abort the drop!" He turned to his microphone.

"Don't." Maurtan pulled his right hand from behind his back; it held a welding laser, the sort used to repair heavy engine shielding.

He leveled it at Hersil. "Turn around, Bif. Walk toward the door."

Hersil did not budge. He stared at the tool-turned-weapon, then at Maurtan's eyes, as though trying to measure his resolve.

"Come on—be sensible, and do what I say!" Ston demanded. "No room in here for another hero."

Without a word, Bif Hersil walked toward the door. Ston paced behind him, hand steady on the torch, marching him into an empty observation room adjoining the control room. "You'll be safe here." He stepped back, shut the door, turned the torch on the door lock. Metal fused under the blue laser light, sealing the door, imprisoning Hersil inside.

He wasn't keeping or making any friends these days, he thought as he re-entered the control room. Moving to the console, he searched out the proper buttons, pressed them. He checked the chronometer again. 3:03.

Switching the torch up full, he aimed for the window, depressed the firing stud. The transparent plastic melted and burned, pouring so much noxious smoke into the room that it was necessary to hold his breath until he was finished.

Taking off his uniform vest, he laid it across the hot, blackened metal sill of the frame, then climbed through. He let himself down to hang by his hands a moment, then dropped five meters to the hangar bay floor.

Mora, disguised in the ensign's uniform, nearly bald head covered with a cap, was waiting on a hangar door, beside the dangling bulk of the Mark IV. After struggling up from the sprawl he had under-taken to break his fall, he hurried over to her.

"Studied one of these babies as a class project at the academy. Old things—don't use them much any more," he said. "I know them in-side and out. Ah—here we go." His fingers found the imbedded but-tons, tapped loose the lock. "Quick, get in. Only a matter of seconds before this place is depressurized, and the doors open underneath us."

Mutely she obeyed, moving through the small opening. Ston crammed himself inside with her, reached out, closed the hatch, twisted hard, sealing it. He fought back the sudden wave of claus-trophobia that engulfed him—they'd conditioned him against that in space training, but fear was eroding the conditioning. Mora was al-ready moving into the cabin, dragging the bag about her neck with her. She set the satchel of food and supplies down, slumped into the acceleration bunk, breathing hoarsely.

Ston keyed closed the optional airlock section—no modern ships had them—and surveyed the inner ship quickly. A small enclosure, all right—but it would have to do. From the looks of it, much of the interior had been in use for quite a while.

Wasting no time, he moved up to the control couch, strapped himself in. "You'd better wrap yourself around something. When the launch dumps us, we'll be moving almost directly into free-fall." His eyes moved over the old control board. Satisfied that all looked well, he checked for a flight computer. Then he recalled the Mark IV's didn't have such—only an environmental computer and a simple automatic course corrector. This journey would have to be all manual.

He tapped on the power. Needles quivered into life—lights blinked on. Primitive, yes—but it worked. It would get them where he planned to go.

The ship rocked slightly. Depressurization had begun.

He turned around to Mora. "I think there's a harness there—yes, slip it on, huh? Only a minute or so until drop time."

"Can't they stop us, if they find out?" she returned as she found the leatherlike straps Ston had indicated, fitted them around herself.

"No. The program's already locked in. I fixed it so that now that hangar deck and its control room aren't accessible. They won't be until they can close the door again. Which they won't be able to do unless we've been ejected. All of which gives us plenty of time to shift into Null-R, and get the hell out of here. We've got a chance, Mora." He turned his warming gaze on her. "We've got a damned good chance now."

"I'm not sure if I care," she said in a small voice. "I just want to get away—make the *effort*." She returned his gaze. "Ston—so far I've been just accepting everything you've done. I suppose I'm still a bit out of it. But I haven't asked you why. Why are you giving up everything for me, Ston?"

A damned good question, he thought. But he had to . . .

Any response he intended was abruptly curtailed by a jerk as the robot cranes began to lower the messenger ship through the open hangar doors, through the artificial gravity field. The Mark IV bumped and lurched. Ston felt as though something was attempting to tear loose inside his body. Mark IV's didn't have anti-grav devices to compensate . . .

And then the ship was tossed out into the void.

"What?" The captain's voice was uncharacteristically shrill. His cup of coffee was spilled as he stood up from the table. Caught in a moment of fury and indecision, he trembled. "Escaped from the *ship*? But who could have helped her?"

A look of fright and paranoia flashed briefly over his features.

Midshipman First Class Ronner stood in semi-rigid attention, eyes straight ahead, enunciating his words precisely. "Security's found Ensign Bifford Hersil in one of the observation rooms. The door had been welded shut. He claims that Ensign Ston Maurtan is responsible."

"Maurtan? Never heard of him. But why, Ronner? Why?"

"Your presence and decisions are requested on the bridge."

"Of course. They'll have to be brought back," he declared. "God knows, I forgot about that messenger ship being slated for ejection, or I would have taken precautions. Someone should have reminded me. This is not a ship—it's a damned bureaucracy. Things will be changed. Now, Ronner—get me an engineering report on that ship right away."

"I already have, Captain." And Ronner's stiff expression turned into a smile.

As the Mark IV hurled away from the huge starship, Mora clung to a handhold, eyes clenched shut. Suddenly, she was weightless, her body straining lightly against the lengths of straps that held her on the bunklike bed. She craned her neck around awkwardly. Ston was muttering over the controls. He grunted with satisfaction as a dim, badly composed picture resolved into shape on the flat screen. "Garbage, all right," he said, beginning to fiddle with something else. She stared past him into the star-spattered blackness. Shining brightly to the left of the screen were the two blazing globes of the Aldebaran system. Even on the flickering black and white screen, the sight was majestic, beautiful. And deadly.

She felt suspended in an ambivalence, not entirely sure if dying was that bad, if one died on one's own terms. But she wanted to live . . .

"Damned chemical engines!" growled Ston. He pounded a control in anger. There was the sudden hiss and clanking of responding machinery. The ship jolted, and Mora could feel a slight measure of gravity again. Its tugging was not unpleasant—an old, familiar friend.

"Well, at least the retros are working," said Ston, almost to himself. "Damned little fuel in the tanks. Day's worth at most. Enough to get us to the colony's shuttle station once we break out of Null-R."

"Ston?" she asked quietly. "What's going to happen?"

"Ah, Mora." He turned around, gave her a comforting smile. "Once I plot the course, we're going to switch on the Null-R engines they so conveniently tacked on for Div's journey."

"But where—?"

"I've got that all figured out," he said. "There's a colony relatively close—Wilkinson's Planet. I think they'll give us haven. You can start a new life, there."

"But what about you, Ston?"

"I'm sure they'll have need for someone with my training and knowledge. I'll have a new life as well. Probably a better one, at that." He swiveled back to the controls. "But I'd better see to adjusting this boat's direction to align with the star-chart figures I copied down. No telling how soon it will be before the *Pegasus* sends a shuttle after us—or comes herself."

"Do you think they'd follow us into Null-R?"

"How are they going to determine either our direction or our destination?" he replied, attending to the instruments. "This is going to be tricky, though. Fairly old equipment. But I think we can pull it off."

Lapsing into silence, he busied himself setting dials, tapping the course-plot keyboard, occasionally consulting the co-ordinates that popped up on a small TV screen at his elbow.

She didn't want to interrupt him. Evidently he knew what he was about. She unstrapped her harness, began to store the supplies—food, water, first-aid equipment—that Ston had packed into the large bag in the available cabinet space. Everything about the cabin looked particularly bare.

A blue light blinked on the console. A crackle rattled in the radio speaker grille, forming into words: ". . . please return immediately lest appropriate action is necess—"

With a brusque jerk, Ston flipped the radio off. "Well, they've got a tab on us now. We've got to move fast. God knows, they might even use the laser-deflectors." He halted the sentence, backed away from that thought. "Now. I've got the course all prepared, punched in. All we've got to do is to drop into Null-R. You ready?"

"Yes. Should I strap in?"

"Probably better. You never know."

She reassumed her former position on the bed. This was it. If they made this jump into Null-R, everything would be okay.

She kept telling herself that.

She closed her eyes, preparing for the jostle of the jump, the lurch into non-relative space.

Nothing happened.

She waited seconds, minutes. She opened her eyes, peered around to Ston at the controls. "What—" she started to say. She stopped when she saw him.

Beads of sweat had popped out on his brow. His eyes were fixed ahead in dull shock. "No," he whispered, "I don't believe it." He turned to face her. "There's no response."

"Are the engines dead?"

He shook his head numbly. "I don't even think they're there at all."

EIGHT

Ston wriggled back into the Mark IV's cabin, shutting the engine access hatch behind him. Frustration was etched on his face. "I should have known," he muttered, sliding into the pilot's chair. "Engineering cannibalized the engines. The parts they must have thought they could use—the Null-R drive's resonating crystal, the jump circuits—they're gone." He stared morosely through the forward viewport. "And I thought I was so goddamned smart."

There was a long silence—the sort of silence that made the faint throbbings and hums of the life-support machinery audible. Mora found herself curiously unshaken at the news. It wasn't like wanting to cry with no tears left. She felt no emotion at all. "What now?" Her words flowed easily, unstrained by worry. "Will they send a shuttle after us?"

Ston twisted around, regarded her. "Maybe. That is, if they want us back. You know, they just might let us—float away. They know we're not going anywhere."

She frowned. "I don't think Darsen would allow that."

"Well, and why *not*? He sure as hell didn't have any qualms whatsoever about having you Doped," he reminded her loudly. His voice lowered suddenly, his gaze softened. "Must say, though—you're taking all this very well."

She gave him a wry smile. "I'm no worse off now than I was in MedSec. Better off, actually. If you hadn't helped me—well, I suppose you know. I'd belong to the ranks of the living dead. They'd have stuck me in some institution back on Earth—finally conformed to their concepts of a co-operative citizen. Thank you."

Ston chuckled. "You're very welcome. But thanks for what? In a few hours you'll probably be back on that operating table."

"Maybe. But if I get a chance, I'll kill myself. I won't surrender quietly—and that's the important thing, isn't it?"

"Not much to lose now for me, either, I suppose." Ston heaved a resigned sigh. He smiled grimly, began miming the act of a popular 3-D entertainer. "I gambled. I lost. I can see the croupier's stick coming forward to scrape my chips off the table."

"And what *were* those chips, Ston?" she asked in a quiet voice, suspecting already. Years of dedication to the service, to his career. His position in the ship's society. Most likely the affection of his friends. All this to help a woman he barely knew? Mora didn't understand—but it made this man's sacrifice all the more significant for her.

He looked up and shrugged. "I forget already." And he smiled bleakly.

The ship's private communicator whistled shrilly. He leaned over, thumbed the speaker switch open, let the beamed message pour out. "—calling Mark IV messenger ship. Triunion starship *Pegasus* calling Mark IV. Please acknowledge, Mr. Maurtan . . ."

Ston picked up the mike, pressed a button. "Here we are, *Pegasus.*"

COMMUNICATIONS LOG
STARSHIP *PEGASUS*—frequency 488823

1101 hours to 1105 hours
Spool 14A4b—Section 4C—Computer
Partial Text
Captain Edan Darsen—bridge, *Pegasus*
Ensign Ston Maurtan—Mark IV messenger ship

DARSEN: I don't know why you have done this, Mr. Maurtan, but I suggest that you co-operate completely.

MAURTAN: I have a formal complaint, Captain. Why was no mention made in the engineering report on this bolt-bucket that you gutted the goddamned Null-R engine? This will look very bad on your record, Captain, I must warn you.

DARSEN: I don't find your remarks humorous, Mr. Maurtan. We are sending out a shuttle to pick you up and tow you back. The motives for your apparent lapse of reason will be discussed once you return. I repeat, it is of the highest importance that you co-operate.

MAURTAN: I want to call my lawyer.

DARSEN: Your rights will be acknowledged, Mr. Maurtan—
            but there are no lawyers aboard the *Pegasus*.

MAURTAN: Hey—how come you want us back so badly? It can't
            be me. I'm not that important. It must be my fel-
            low passenger here, Mora Elbrun, mustn't it? It'll
            look bad for you if anything happens to her. Is that
            it? What if I told you that she's my hostage, and
            that I expect a good deal of ransom if you expect
            her back in one piece.

DARSEN: I don't believe you understand the seriousness of
            your offense, Ensign. Your levity will be ignored if
            you simply signal willingness to co-operate.

MAURTAN: Screw you, sir.

DARSEN: What do you mean by—

MAURTAN: Okay, listen up, Captain. I'm onto you now. Some-
            thing's happening. You don't need me—but you
            need Mora, right? Unless you deliver her totally
            Doped to the Tricouncil, you're in hot water, right?
            They've got to have their sacrifice. Well, I'll make
            a deal, Captain. There's no way you can stop me if
            I want to just let all that airless space inside this
            ship. If I did that, you wouldn't have much to bring
            back, would you?

DARSEN: You wouldn't do that, damn you.

MAURTAN: Wouldn't I? Mora wouldn't mind. She knows
            what's waiting for her back on board your ship—

DARSEN: I assure you, Ensign, that the psychemicidian treat-
            ments will be stopped.

MAURTAN: You took the words out of my mouth. It's a deal.
            I assume this is going into the communications
            computer, so you're going to have to stick to it.

DARSEN: Your little escapade was purposeless, Mr. Maurtan.
            If you had checked with MedSec, you would have
            seen that I had ordered the treatments stopped even

before you abducted the subject. When you get back, I'll show you a copy.

MAURTAN: Oh.

Ston pointed out a tiny moving star in the mostly black of the vu-plate. "There's the shuttle. All we have to do is wait, now."

She stood by him, her hands on his shoulders. "Your muscles are in knots," she said, closing her eyes, trying to feel what he felt. Nothing came to her—not via her Talent, anyway.

"It's called 'tension.' I can't *believe* it was all for nothing. It makes me feel pretty stupid."

"You mean you really believe Darsen?"

"I guess so."

"Even if he *is* telling the truth, it doesn't take away one bit of your heroism, Ston. And it means every bit as much to me."

He glanced up at her and changed the subject. "It must be strange to you, not being able to read my emotions."

"It is," she agreed. "But it's a relief, in a way."

"Will it come back?"

"My Talent? Probably. One injection is hardly enough to dampen it permanently. And when it comes, it comes. It's almost as though it were a freakish deformity that I'm not able to deal with entirely, but I do accept."

Ston's eyes searched hers with displeasure. "*Never* say that, Mora. A Talent isn't a monkey-on-the-back, like you seem to think it is."

She smiled slightly, curiously. This was a clue to his motivation in helping her—for his interest and concern with her unique nature. She tried to pry it out of him gently. "Most Normals wouldn't say that to me. You've had other contact with Talents?"

"My sister was a Talent," he replied quietly. "She died. A suicide."

"I'm sorry. Were you close to her?"

He looked away, nodding silently. His eyes followed the silent sailing light of the shuttle, coming for them.

She realized that she didn't need her Talent to read this man. The slight gleam of moisture in his eyes, the manner in which he held his head, the way his jaw worked, swallowing his emotions, said it all.

She watched him awhile, then asked, "How far away is the shuttle?"

Ston, yanked from his reverie, was startled. "Hmmm? Oh." He

checked some instruments. "Fifty thousand kilometers or so. It will take a little while."

Gently, she touched his arm. "Ston. I think I understand."

"Do you? Even without the Talent? Thanks." He peered up into her eyes. "Yes—and I'm beginning to understand, too. But not everything. We have some time. I'd like to know what happened with Darsen on the bridge. I want to know everything about *Tin Woodman* you can tell me. It's something that I can see in you—it's very important, isn't it?"

She thought back on it—and even as she did she felt the faint echoing thrill of the experience, which in its reverberations carried new meaning and the promise of more to come. But how could she possibly communicate the vision that Div had given her so briefly, so that she might tell Ston? Suddenly, in that moment, she had been whisked from the *Pegasus'* bridge. She had been, momentarily, a creature of the spaces between the stars, in flight through a universe of perfect, unbounded freedom and joy. Somehow, with Div as a link, she had glimpsed the truth of *Tin Woodman*. And the stars had stretched out before her, as they must have for Div, like toys awaiting the marvel of a child . . .

There was more—much more—that she had no way of understanding. But perhaps she would. Soon.

"Yes," she said. "Yes, I believe it is very important."

She told Ston everything she could.

There was so much beyond his comprehension, although it was a part of his mind, now. Back aboard the *Pegasus*, as soon as he had established peripheral contact with the ship-being they called *Tin Woodman*, Div knew that to obey Darsen in his wishes was not part of the plan. But what exactly that plan was, he had no way of knowing then. He only felt a jumble of emotions within him—the drive to get closer to the alien, and the need to be sure that Edan Darsen was not able to control the creature through him. He didn't think rationally, then; indeed he wondered now if he had been in control of himself at all, rather than acting on the dictates of a greater consciousness.

But Div realized that it was vital to understand, for things of importance loomed in the gray, veiled areas of his new identity.

What exactly *was* his new identity? He wondered, aware of the steady thrum of the engines as they drove the ship-being forward in Null-R. He replayed his memory again . . .

The corridor is long, with many intersections, but the voice within him beckons him onward, and he feels a slow change take root in his soul as he goes forward, committed now to this quest.

Finally, he enters a large bright chamber: curved walls, gleaming metal, glistening crystal, pulsing light. A chair—no, not a chair, nothing like a chair, but a resting place nonetheless. He senses, perhaps through contact with the alien, that this place is memory-haunted; this was where Vul lived, during the long journeys through interstellar space.

Vul, the dead symbiote. The necessary other part of Tin Woodman. The love without which the ship-being waned.

But now, it had Div.

COME TO ME. SIT.

Div does so without fear or hesitation, closing his eyes. He reaches out even more with his mind, searching, opening himself, surrendering his spirit.

And meets the alien, fully.

Creation seems to shatter—the tiny little multi-colored sounds spiraling/scattering senseless in the vacuum of space. All that the two creatures have been tumble aimlessly in shards, re-forming slowly and painstakingly, toward the eventual rebuilding of a new, random creature that would be both and yet neither. The mind fragments soar, begin to yield to the thoughts, feelings, fears, and dreams and hopes and memories of the other parts.

And yet the fragments are distinguishable.

"This is the beginning of our love," Tin Woodman says. "Eventually, the pieces will meld, become one. A new creation, and a new being, will be totally born at last. Our consciousness will expand to feel the whole of space. We will be complete. We will be I. The emptiness that held me prisoner about that star system for so long is being filled. The Talent that separated you from your fellow humans all of your life is being fulfilled. You have found the chains that will set you free."

"And yet," the part of him that was becoming *Tin Woodman* broke into his memory replay, "this is nothing that will happen quickly. Do not be concerned. The fact that you are not totally like Vul's kind is a barrier that must be slowly surmounted. Understanding will come, soon enough, and you will see what we have done, what we are doing, and what is to be done. It is all one. There is much to teach you, and much for you to learn."

"You prevented Darsen from harming me, through Mora. You gave her that power."

"We both did. And we both have done other things—then. There has been a reason for every motion you made, every thought you had from the moment you felt my existence. The results of what we have done are not finished yet—*you* have seen to that."

"Me?"

"We, now."

"But how?"

"Reach out. Reach out into space, and *experience*. It is all written in the cosmic energy flows."

Div reached out with the arms of his mind that *Tin Woodman* had given him, into the energy.

"Soon, you will understand. And we will be complete," said *Tin Woodman*, and Div realized that these thoughts were beginning to feel like his own.

Edan Darsen slouched back into his command desk chair and rubbed his big hand down the side of his face, feeling the light stubble of his beard. Underneath the hand and stubble he was aware that an angry flush painted his broad face. He sucked in a breath and let it out raggedly, calming himself. His ability to command must not be questioned if he hoped to succeed in what he intended to do. And his intentions, after all, were of paramount importance—so important that he was willing to forego his vengeance upon Mora Elbrun for now to succeed in them.

He stood. It was better, now. He had Mora back now, he told himself. Stupid of him to order that first psychemicidian treatment so hastily. But in a way that would be useful now—she *knew* what they were like, and the threat of further treatments could be a factor in his favor. She was the key . . . the link. If they could tap her, as Tamner had suggested they might . . .

There he was—stiff and alert in his seat next to the sensor console. "Tamner?"

"Yes, sir." Tamner rose to attention perfectly, yet with no grace of movement.

"Mr. Tamner, you are relieved of duties unrelated to our present project until further notice. The experiment will be accorded the utmost priority—your work is of great importance."

"Thank you, Captain."

Briskly, Darsen leaned over his desk and punched out a code on his intercom controls.

"Security. Lieutenant Abriel," erupted a voice immediately.

"Captain Darsen here. I have just spoken to our fugitives, Lieutenant. Orders are presently being dispatched to the shuttle craft on proper handling once the recapture is effected. I don't expect trouble, but be ready for it should it come. Most important is that the woman, Mora Elbrun, is *not* harmed, whatever may happen. She is to be taken to her quarters and placed under guard there until further notice. She should have no visitors unless I am present. As for that man, Maurtan . . ." His voice turned hard. "Stick him in the brig. Make him uncomfortable—for the interim, until we can bring up proceedings against him."

"Yes, Captain."

Satisfied, Darsen flicked the intercom off, feeling more composed already. This was as a starship should be run. Captain? Yes, captain. With the captain's permission. . . . Discipline, organization, obedience: without these, the crew of the *Pegasus* could not function together properly toward one goal. That this goal would be a personal one for Edan Darsen did not trouble him.

Yes. Perhaps he had mismanaged himself before. But now that he had a definite purpose in mind, he found it easier to moderate his fiery temper. And without that temper, he knew he had more respect from the crew. Respect, obedience, and efficiency would be rewarded. There would be glory enough for all if everything worked well. And Edan Darsen intended for things to work very well indeed.

Tamner was a good example of the sort of co-operation he needed. The first image that had come to him upon recovery of consciousness was that of Jin Tamner, standing by him—on guard against any further attacks. They had talked later and found much in common. And Tamner was sharp—very sharp. It was Tamner who had perceptively analyzed the potential meaning of what had happened with *Tin Woodman*—and it was Tamner who had suggested the course of action that Darsen had settled upon.

A brilliant man. He had been a research technician for Triplanetary Holo-Acoustical Communications Incorporated before he had joined the service. He had given Darsen the means by which he could see that this business with the alien was not yet over.

Tamner was a good officer. Tamner would not be forgotten once this affair was done with.

Tamner. He had to discuss something with him immediately. But he had been relieved . . .

A quick sweep of his gaze found him standing by the lift. "Ah, Tamner. I'm glad you're not gone."

An obedient jerk of his neck: Tamner nodded curtly, jostling his thick thatch of perfectly styled hair. "You did not give permission to leave the bridge, Captain. And I thought you might wish—"

"Yes." He looked at him thoughtfully. Tamner's face was expressionless. *Tamner* had no problem keeping his emotions in check—if he had any emotions at all. "Yes, Tamner. You're quite right. With all this commotion of late, we've not had the opportunity to discuss the apparatus you've devised. I thought we might get down to it. Hungry?"

"Yes, Captain."

"Good. I sure am. We'll talk in the mess hall." He looked over to where Norlan sat. "Lieutenant Norlan, I'm taking a break; you have command. Call Lieutenant Garyve to relieve you at the communications console."

"Yes, Captain," Norlan replied, immediately carrying out the order.

A different sort from Tamner, this Norlan, thought Darsen. Both good men—but Norlan had opposed him at that briefing. Technically he had been within his rights—but it was a displeasure to Darsen nonetheless. Well, a certain amount of friction among the officers was to be expected, sometimes. The fellow would simply have to learn that *Darsen's* authority aboard ship was absolute. He would come around.

And if not—well, he could easily be replaced.

When they reached the mess hall, it was practically deserted.

Tamner ordered a full meal. Darsen selected oddments of fruit and a pot of coffee. His hands full with the tray, he nodded Tamner toward an officers' alcove. He didn't want their conversation to be overheard.

"Have you had any difficulty finding the equipment you need for your device?" Darsen asked, taking a sip of his coffee.

After hastily gulping down his mouthful of food, Tamner said, "Between MedSec and engineering stores I've been able to do it. The doctors don't like my taking over their precious holo-scanner."

Darsen shrugged. "If you need it, use it. I certainly don't understand this well enough to second-guess you, and neither do they."

"They understand it well enough. They just don't like it. The principles of the memory scanner aren't that new. It works, basically, by energetic stimulation of certain brain areas. In this case, we've found a way to use coherent sound energy for that purpose."

Darsen frowned. "If it's so simple—"

"Why hasn't it been done?" Tamner finished for him. "As I said, in *principle* it's simple. But think: we're trying to find one particular piece of information which is buried in Mora Elbrun's subconscious memory. We need computer equipment to rapidly evaluate and reject everything that comes to the surface except what we're looking for. This in itself is complicated to set up. Beyond this, we need Elbrun's co-operation."

"Then this device can't be used on a person against his will."

"If necessary, it can—but it's dangerous and takes much longer. If Elbrun *wants* to remember, she can sift her memory faster than the computers can. Machines have their limitations. Without her co-operation we'd need a medical technician familiar with interrogation drugs."

"Has the memory scanner ever been used that way?"

"Well . . . THC had us work the procedure out. Galactic Command wanted to use it on Goridan during the rebellion."

"Did they?"

"I really don't know. Wasn't my affair. Brass just told me to develop the damned thing. I did, I got paid—including a percentage of patent royalties, which have been meager so far. I'm surprised you aren't familiar with it."

"No. I had other things to think about during that time. I have to admit, though, I don't much like the principle of this device. Too much like telepathy for my taste. I don't know about you, Tamner, but reading minds to me is a fundamental invasion of human privacy. I regard those that exercise these talents as moral criminals."

"I could not agree with you more," responded Tamner quickly. "But that would not quite be the case here. This is much more primitive than telepathy. If anything, it should be easier to use on Elbrun, if she co-operates. She's primed for it, you might say. But then again, she does have the blocks and barriers that all espers develop. As for your hesitancy—I'm sure the end will justify the means."

"Of course," said Darsen. "As for those blocks you mentioned, Elbrun won't use them. She'll co-operate."

"Well, whatever you say. But it's a shame you have to bargain with her for that co-operation." His eyes took on a fiery aspect; a flicker of emotion beneath the cool exterior. "She's *dangerous*. Even under an injection of psychemicidian she managed to get this Maurtan to help attempt an escape."

Darsen found his jaw muscles tightening involuntarily. His voice was terse. "Yes. I agree. I have personal experience with the danger in her, as you may recall. I'd just as soon blank her, or toss her out into deep space without a suit. I do wish I knew exactly what happened. As far as I can tell, they didn't even know one another. I don't care to bargain with her, Tamner. But as you say, her co-operation will speed the discovery of the information we need on *Tin Woodman*. Obtaining that information is of paramount importance."

Tamner finished his last forkful of food thoughtfully, then pushed away his tray. "Why?"

Darsen sipped the cooling coffee. It was bitter. He was acutely aware of the silence about him that rendered his thoughts quite stark. He had mentioned to Tamner before about what he had heard had happened after Mora Elbrun had attacked him. There was no doubt that Mora had been somehow in contact with *Tin Woodman* then—and it was Tamner who had suggested the method by which they might extract the exact memory from her for the details they needed. But Tamner did not suspect what he was all too sure was the truth; as in Mora, though to a lesser extent, there were memories —an experience, buried in his mind, and the minds of the entire crew—planted there by this alien creature.

He knew his own mind quite well. There had been nightmares . . .

"There are several reasons, Tamner. All good ones. Why not just forget about the whole thing and be about our business, you ask. Let me ask you something first, Tamner. Do you like Talents?"

The man's grimace was sufficient reply.

"No," Darsen said. "Nor I. I've never liked them. I truly do not believe that they are a normal growth in the development of mankind. They are freaks; they have no place in mankind's history. Perhaps they have their own destiny. God knows. But I don't want them messing about in our destiny, *our* ideals for the future. Mankind is only as strong as each of its individuals—we must train ourselves to rely only on our own inner resources. To be no one but ourselves, forge our own individual destinies, take charge of our own lives. This is the lesson of natural selection; and the lesson each of us should listen to, for it comes from within. But the Talents? They're trying to defeat the individual—two or more of them together, and you've got a conspiracy against individuality—theirs *and* ours. Take the behavior of Div Harlthor and Mora Elbrun—and yes, *Tin Woodman* too. They tried to *kill* me! And I know they would have if they could. I know. They're different, Tamner; a sinister difference. From the beginning I got the impression of conspiracy—which was shown to be true with their team effort to foul up contact with the alien. And that creature—it must have a Talent—and much more. But maybe people like Elbrun and Harlthor have more in common with that alien than they do with *us*. Therefore, I see that alien, in conjunction with these 'Talents,' as we call them, as definitely hostile not only to the Triunion, but to the future of individuality in man. Why else did it, in conjunction with Elbrun and Harlthor, react in such a way when it awoke?"

"I see what you mean."

"Yes. It would be of utmost service to the Triunion and to the human race to find this creature before it finds others of its kind. Find it and *destroy* it before it notifies them of our existence—and the existence of the Talents within our midst."

"There's more, though, isn't there, Darsen?"

Darsen nodded solemnly. "Yes."

"You want revenge."

"A poor enough word, but it will do."

Tamner let a smile creep up on his face. "And you want redemption, don't you, Captain Darsen. You want power for your particular rugged individuality."

Darsen frowned. "Well, man. What do *you* want?"

"Everything I can get."

Darsen grinned. "Excellent. It's good to know I'm working with my own kind."

But Darsen did not mention to the man the other reason that gnawed in him. It would be impossible to make Tamner understand; not without revealing in full what he could hardly bear to remember: that moment when Mora had driven her mind into his—

and he knew that it was more than just *her* mind. For it was as if he had been swept from the bridge of the starship into a sudden surging feeling of defenselessness, nakedness. As though he had been hurled, unprotected, toward the distant stars. He had felt his soul open to the penetrating gaze of the universe and all its creatures.

Upon recovery of consciousness, he did not remember the experience. It must have taken place in a fraction of a second. Even now, during his waking hours, the memory was like an ancient, half-buried guilt, a fluttering movement at the periphery of his mind's eye's range. In darkness, in sleep, the memory returned, clothed as nightmare.

No, it was not merely out of a desire for vengeance that Edan Darsen wished to pursue *Tin Woodman*. Nor was it out of simple desire for redemption and glory in the eyes of the Triunion. Darsen hated *Tin Woodman*. Hated it because he feared it. Feared it because of what it had revealed to him.

PART THREE:

THE PURSUIT

"Foreboding shivers ran over me.
Reality outran apprehensions;
Captain Ahab stood upon his quarter-deck."

—Herman Melville

MOBY DICK

NINE

They were extraordinarily civil to her.

She had expected to be mishandled much in the same manner as when Security had hauled her away from the scene of Captain Darsen's injury. Instead, once the shuttle had docked with the Mark IV messenger ship and towed it back to the *Pegasus*, the security officers stationed there had stepped forward smartly when the hangar deck was depressurized and had *asked* her please to accompany them. No force—nor even a show of it.

However, Ston—who immediately let it be known that his laser welding device had been abandoned in the Mark IV—was brusquely jostled away with no attention at all paid to his comfort.

They had exchanged one last look, and he was gone.

Now she sat in her comfortable, well-decorated compartment, with a tray of somewhat exotic refreshments on the table before her. Even before Darsen and Tamner entered the room, she had concluded that something was desired of her.

Once inside, the captain looked about, nodded his head with satisfaction. There was a strained look on his sturdy face—a faint hint of fear, kept well in check. Fear—yes, and hate. "Very nice," he said. "I hope everything is all right." He made an attempt at a smile that failed. Then he said, in a quiet, gruff voice, "There are two security guards at the door, Mora. I hope you will do nothing to upset them."

"I know." She shifted uncomfortably on the edge of her bed, not looking at Darsen but glaring at Jin Tamner, who leaned smugly against the wall next to her cabin door. She had sensed the guards' presence since they had been placed there. But that was all she sensed. Still, it proved that her Talent was slowly returning. "I don't want that man in here," she declared, standing abruptly. "If you wish to speak with me, get Tamner out of here."

Tamner opened his mouth to protest, but Darsen motioned for silence. "You have no authority on this ship, Elbrun," he replied brusquely. "You can demand nothing."

"And you can't force me to do anything, either," she returned vehemently.

Folding his arms on his chest, Darsen nodded, then turned to Tamner. "Wait in the hall."

Unquestioning, Tamner exited with a sullen, guarded look at Mora. She was grateful her Talent had not returned in significant force; she couldn't feel his hatred.

Not until the door slid fully shut did Darsen continue. "I'm not going to play games with you, Elbrun. You put yourself between me and what I wanted, and you harmed me. I cannot forgive you for that, nor do I need to."

"I did what I had to do, Darsen."

"Shall we simply ignore the past for now, Elbrun? In a way, you can make up for what you have done by co-operating with me." Darsen refused to relax. He stood there, his arms folded, stiff, resolute.

"What can *I* do to help *you*? I'm certainly not going to be the *Pegasus'* shiplady again." Sound cool, unconcerned, she told herself. She looked down. Her hands were trembling. They gave her away.

Sighing, she ran her hand over the stubble covering her head, wincing inwardly at the thought of how she looked. When gently imprisoned in the room, she'd caught her reflection in a mirror; a scarecrow's corpse in a baggy, rumpled engineering uniform. Her eyes were sunken and hollow, set in a worn, sallow face. The blond fuzz sprouting unevenly on her scalp gave her the appearance of a prison camp refugee.

She had covered the mirror immediately.

It wasn't vanity. It was just that now she was not merely different from everyone else; now she *looked* different. She did not care to be reminded of her recent experiences.

"Settle down, Elbrun," ordered Darsen. "I'm not going to hurt you."

Mora leaned back, still tense.

"I don't enjoy talking to you. I know you don't like talking with me. I will be blunt and quick." He shifted his massive bulk slightly from foot to foot. "I've been thinking, Elbrun. You alone could not have hurt me like you did. I've been looking over your records. You have never exhibited such powers before, nor do any tests reveal them. *Tin Woodman* guided your hand, so to speak. Am I correct? Were you in contact with the alien?"

She did not answer immediately. Darsen took it as a refusal to talk.

"Well?" he demanded impatiently.

"I don't know. I . . . I must have been, to have that power . . . and later . . . yes, definitely later." She looked away. Was she betraying Div?

"Very good, Mora. We are being honest with one another. Very good indeed." The bastard was starting to sound *cordial*. "That final communication you speak of—that was from both *Tin Woodman* and Div Harlthor, wasn't it? I know—because I think I felt it as well. Even though I was unconscious. . . . Perhaps we all felt it, at a subconscious level. Maybe it was merely the effect of his contact with you. Now, if your link with Div and *Tin Woodman* was strong and deep enough, it may very well be that you've received information from them of which you are consciously unaware—information buried in your subconscious mind, which can be useful to the Triunion."

"What kind of information?"

The captain leaned forward. "Perhaps *Tin Woodman*'s intended destination . . . ?" Something about that tone of voice. Intense. Obsessed. It bothered Mora in a way she couldn't put her finger on.

"That information is certainly not in my conscious mind. But all right. Suppose it's somewhere below that. If it is, I certainly can't get at it."

"All I want you to do, Mora, all you need to do to become vital personnel once more—to be absolved of your sins, shall we say—is to assist in an experiment."

"And if I don't, I get sent back to the machines and the surgeons, right?" Mora said uneasily.

"Yes," stated Darsen. "I would have no—"

"Spare me." Despite her bitterness, Mora was tempted to accept the man's proposal as it stood. Surely no harm could be done Div by aiding Darsen; the *Pegasus* could chase *Tin Woodman* halfway across the galaxy and never catch it. The pursuit would be given up long before then; Darsen was far too sensible to do otherwise.

Nevertheless, she couldn't accept.

Not without a stipulation.

"If I agree to your 'experiment,' it will only be under one condition. There's something I want in exchange."

"I'm practically giving you your *life* in exchange," said Darsen. "You're in no bargaining position."

"No? You seem to want this information I'm supposed to have rather badly. All right then. I'll co-operate if and only if you'll release Ston Maurtan. I presume he's in the brig."

Darsen was indignant. "*Out* of the question. He's committed mutinous acts—he must face the consequences."

In response, Mora waved a hand over the access control panel by her bed. The cabin door opened. She politely motioned for Darsen to leave.

The captain's voice became cold steel. "You can be forced."

"If that's true, why did you ask in the first place? You'd just as soon have me out of the way, wouldn't you? I *scare* you, Captain."

Darsen remained immobile a moment. The veins in the thick neck stood out. A swallow bobbed the Adam's apple. Then he said, "Very well. We will compromise. I will offer Maurtan the chance to resign his commission. If he accepts, the charges against him will be dropped. I'll free him, and he'll be considered a passenger—subject to the customary passenger restrictions aboard the ship."

Quietly, Mora said, "Thank you."

"At 0800 hours you will report to MedSec," Darsen said, ignoring the apology implicit in Mora's voice. "You will co-operate fully with Dr. Kervatz and Lieutenant Tamner. And you will hold yourself available for *further* such experiments if they are deemed necessary. Understood?"

"Yes."

"Good." Without another word, Darsen spun on his heel and stalked out.

After shutting the door, Mora collapsed on her bed. Exhaustion overwhelmed her, bringing its usual attendant, depression. All of it had worn her down. The strain of the treatment. Her recovery. The escape. And now, the confrontation.

It was difficult to believe she'd done it: stood up to the captain. And won. But there was no feeling of satisfaction in her.

Sleep came suddenly and brought no dreams.

Ship's time was adjusted to align with the day-night cycle shared by all the planets of the Triunion: 0800 hours fell into the time slot immediately following "night." So it was that when Mora, accompanied by the present pair of security officers posted at her door, walked to MedSec it was "morning" although no sun had risen, and the corridors were brightly lit as always.

They were all waiting for her. Kervatz, Tamner, Darsen. Quietly, Kervatz motioned her to a reclining chair. No clamps or restraining straps or other implements of confinement were administered. No anesthesia was given; a simple injection of tranquilizer was deemed sufficient to create the suggestible mood in the subject necessary for a hypnotic trance.

Hypnosis accomplished, Jin Tamner directed the placement of electrodes on her scalp and spine by the attendant nurse; these wires were in turn connected to a bank of recording equipment and computer terminals, modified toward this special procedure. Above Mora's head, a device partly made of the MedSec acoustical holograph tank was set. Microtransmitters were attached to her ears. Once Tamner was satisfied that all was in readiness, he pressed the necessary controls.

Tiny whispers floated up from the attachments in her ears: questions. No verbal reply was requested. To the surrounding witnesses, they were meaningless; no more than sibilant nonsense.

But Tamner seemed pleased.

Watching the shifting patterns in the holo-tank, making minor adjustments to the recorders, he said, "This may take half an hour at most, Captain. But it might be several days before the computers can pick out and supply the information we want."

"If indeed she has it to give," commented Darsen, betraying worry despite himself.

"I thought you were convinced she did," said Tamner. "I would say it's there. Imagine that she has part of Div's—and hopefully *Tin Woodman's*—mind, recorded in her memory. That's what telepathy basically amounts to, after all, in its advanced stages: a sharing of consciousness. The minds involved retain images of one another afterward. Most of the memories remain unconscious ones, and some information is probably lost. But from papers I consulted in helping to perfect this process, I'd say this is pretty much the case.

"What we're trying to get from her, though, is a very specific set of memories—the Null-R jump co-ordinates which *Tin Woodman* was preparing to use when Mora was in contact with Div. So they should be easily retrievable."

"Yet we can hardly expect that *Tin Woodman* uses our co-ordinate system," Darsen objected.

"True, but that's not important. Mora's mind-to-mind experience with the alien by-passes translation difficulties like that. If we were trying to re-create *Tin Woodman*'s whole mind, conflict, traumas, values, and the like, we'd encounter images and ideas which would *not* translate. But just as hydrogen is hydrogen by whatever name you call it, math is math."

"Well, you don't need me here," said Darsen. "I'm going to see to Maurtan's release, then to the bridge. Report to me when you've finished."

"Yes, Captain." Tamner seemed disturbed. "You're really going to release Maurtan?"

"I said I would," he replied, "and I certainly don't wish to feed Elbrun's illusions of persecution. You needn't be concerned though that Maurtan might escape punishment. I've made certain arrangements concerning his release." Darsen turned to Dr. Kervatz. "When our interrogator is through with Elbrun, give her a complete physical examination," he ordered. "I want to make certain, for the record, that she hasn't been harmed by the psychemicidian."

"Very little chance of that, Captain," replied Kervatz.

"Nevertheless, do it." He glanced at the prone figure in the chair, her head freshly shaved to allow attachment of the electrodes. "And give her a hair-stim if she wants one."

A while after they finally released her, Mora found Ston on the observation deck.

Security had told her that he'd been released. She checked both the civilian passenger directory and the old officer listing—he was registered on neither. She'd then searched every public area of the ship and found him at last.

He sat sprawled in a chair beneath a darkened archway. She noticed then the storage trunk, two suitcases, and the shoulder bag lying at his feet. "Ston—you all right?"

He lifted his head with difficulty, as though his neck were rubber. "Yeah. Resigned my commish—commission."

"I heard." She looked for the bottle, saw it standing on the floor: a bulb-shaped green glass bottle, three-quarters empty.

"Yeah. When they booted me, I asked what you'd done to save my ass. They said something about an experiment and that 'she's not available today.' So I thought I'd come up here, watch the stars—"

"And drink."

"Yeah." He lifted the bottle, thrust it unsteadily toward Mora. "Want some?"

Well, if *she* had some, it was that much less that he'd drink. "Sure, why not?" She took the bottle. "Wine?"

"Uh-huh. Good wine, I think. I wouldn't really know. Effective enough, anyway. Found it cleaning out my quarters. A gift . . ." Closing his eyes, he slipped down in his chair, breathing heavily.

Mora sipped the wine. A heavy, rather sweet taste. Amontillado, the label read. "This is sherry. God, how could you drink so much?"

"Easy." He leaned forward and added in a confidential manner, "Don't know any better. I don't drink." He straightened up in his chair, looking serious and apparently trying to will sobriety. "I know —I'm sloshed. Sorry, I couldn't think of anything else to do. Why not? No one on this ship will talk to me anyway."

"Why not?"

" 'Cause I endangered the ship. Drilling holes in the walls around here is *verboten*, y'know. Mortal sin . . . bad manners, too. One might burn through the wrong wall . . ."

"The first thing you should have done," Mora said pragmatically, "was to get another compartment, in the passenger section—"

"Got no money. Service took it all—"

"What?"

"Damage to the ship, Mora," he explained, as if to a dense child. "Darsen billed me for it. Closed my account right out. All I have is what you see before you. Think there's a good conduct medal in that suitcase there—" He stretched forward, reaching for one of the suitcases, and nearly fell on his face. Mora caught him and lifted him to his feet.

"Can you walk?" she asked, angry at Darsen—it would take a mind like his to conceive such a way of reneging on his promise. There wasn't anything officially wrong with holding Ston responsible for damage he'd caused to the *Pegasus*. And the captain wouldn't allow Ston to starve; Ston would simply be forced, after a few days, to let Darsen put him into a Henderson for the duration of the voyage, thus ridding the ship of at least one troublemaker.

Ston was capable of walking, but not in a particular direction. Placing one arm under his shoulders, letting him lean on her, Mora led him onto the lift platform. When they began to drop his face turned pale and Mora was afraid he would be sick.

"My things," he mumbled. "Can't leave them up there."

"No one's going to steal your luggage. I'll go back for it later." The lift halted on Mora's deck, and she led Ston down the corridor to her quarters. When she let go of him to open the door, he staggered and fell against the bulkhead.

"I am wasted!" he announced almost gleefully, attempting without much success to stand up unassisted.

"Another of your old naval expressions? Here—your hand." She pulled him up to his feet, directed him into her darkened quarters, letting him fall onto the bed. As she turned on the bedside light, he tried to raise himself on his elbows.

"I'll sleep in a chair," he said. "Can't put you out of bed."

"Don't be silly. There's room enough for me. You'll feel lousy enough when you wake up." She struggled to pull his vest off, noticing the darker, unworn patches of color where his insignia of rank had so recently been removed. After more struggling, she decided he'd have to sleep in the rest of his uniform.

"I'm not kidding about them not speaking to me, Addy—uh, Mora. Even my friends won't. I've been ostra—osher—rejected."

"They couldn't have been very good friends." With limited assistance from Ston, Mora managed to stretch him out in what looked like a comfortable position.

"Right. Trade 'em all for you any day." His eyes closed.

"Thanks." Staring down at him, a cold scream of fury rose in her mind. If he believed that, it was because he had to. She could feel how it hurt him to be an outcast.

Well, she had enough credits in her own account to provide for him. He wouldn't wind up on sleeper deck—not while she could help him. And what could the captain do about it?

So much for Darsen's dirty trick.

She looked down at Ston. He lay motionless, breathing slowly, easily. Relaxed, his features were smooth in the dim wall light. The hair on his unlined, unshaved face was spare; too fine to be called stubble. So young . . .

In most ways, Div Harlthor had been older than Ston Maurtan. Div was like her; he'd learned the hard way how treacherous people could be toward the vulnerable.

Ston was just beginning to discover that.

He frowned in his sleep. She put a hand on his forehead. He was dreaming. The dream was a bad one. She could feel his disorientation, his fear, even with only the fraction of Talent that had returned.

She took her hand away. His dreams should be his own.

There was a tense, electric charge to the atmosphere on the bridge. Sitting stiffly at his command desk, Captain Edan Darsen knew that he was in the center of it.

All was silent save for the occasional whisper of activity among the crew and the ever-present quiet hum of the computers.

Any moment now, I'll know, he thought, his eyes settled steadfastly upon the form of Lieutenant Tamner, leaning over the main terminal. Any second now the letter-perforated strip of plastic would click out of the mouth of that machine, tongue-like. That tape would either bear the vector co-ordinates of the Null-R jump that *Tin Woodman* had initiated and its destination, or the indication that no such information had been available in the mind of Mora Elbrun.

It would be a single point of time that would determine his destiny.

If there was no information to be had, pursuit of the alien was pointless. The *Pegasus* would continue on its appointed rounds, his life would settle back to its veritable jail sentence—and he would never be satisfied. Always, in the back of his mind, there would be doubt. . . .

But if the result of the mind-pick was positive, then this threat to normal humanity might be found and dealt with—and he could have what he wanted; his chase, his revenge, and his chance for redemption and glory.

A red light on the computer console blipped. The tape began to spew.

He realized that he was standing, expectantly.

Tamner looked up from the tape with a satisfied glint in his eyes. "It's all here, Captain. More than we'd hoped for. Much more."

A thrill of triumph raced through him. "Very well, Mr. Tamner. All is in readiness. There is no time to be wasted." He could feel the strength grow in his voice. "Order more copies of the information immediately and supply the astrogator, the pilots, and other necessary crewmen with those co-ordinates, if you please."

Obediently, Tamner spun on his heel to implement the orders. As he punched in directions on the computer's typeboard, Darsen found himself drifting over toward the lieutenant—no, he would make Tamner lieutenant commander now. He lifted the tape up and looked down on the symbols in something like wonder.

"Null-R engines activated, Captain."

He was back behind the command desk now, infused with purpose. The *Pegasus* was in position. All that remained was to order the jump.

"Commence interlocking procedure," he said.

A quick flutter of the hand of the pertinent pilot.

"Set cycles at previously specified codes."

"Cycles set," responded a pilot.

"Start phasing jump," he commanded, unable to exclude a note of excitement from his voice. "Erect Null-R field."

"Field erected; jump phasing."

Streamers of light began to vortex toward the flat screen from star-salted space. They coiled about the entire field of view, and they were swallowed up in flashing, dancing colors.

"Jump phasing complete. Null-R jump in progress. Speed, Captain?"

"Just short of maximum," he said.

"Yes, Captain."

And the *Pegasus* became a little fish, flashing through the sea of infinity.

Extended into the mega-flow, Div felt a subtle change; a flux. "What causes this?" For some reason, it had echoes of importance.

The creature he was slowly sinking into responded after long moments of analysis in depths of thought Div could not yet pierce. "The metal ship that found me now pursues. It is as we thought it would be—as, perhaps, we planned."

Alarmed, Div drew back into his place of protection. "What? If Darsen is in command, they can only have malevolent intent. Are they capable of catching us—destroying us?"

"All is written in the mega-flow. You must learn to use that—or learn to comprehend it through the growing link between us."

Div reached out again—and noticed another change in the flow. It seemed to emanate from them—and, simultaneously, to be coming from an outside source. He asked *Tin Woodman* the reason for this.

"There are others like us," it/he said. "We have been signaling them since our penetration of what you call 'Null-R space.' They will meet us at the end of this segment of our journey, our pilgrimage as you might say. But you have not been opening up fully, my love. You are a lax student. Prepare yourself—I must show you. Try to surrender the shreds of the will you stubbornly cling to . . ."

And abruptly Div realized that non-relative space felt *different* somehow from normal space. All phenomena seemed to radiate outward from a point infinitely far ahead which grew no closer as *Tin Woodman* moved. Div felt himself moving nonetheless; his consciousness was flung forward, existing in the ever-distant center of the Null-R vortex, even as it was cradled in the body of the ship-being. Somehow, he felt himself *here*, rushing to meet himself *there*.

Radioactive particles poured over them like rain, like sleet stinging his face as he trudged along a noisy road, aware of others ahead.

"This is much like the place where Vul was lost," the ship-being said. "Our protection failed somehow—rains like these poisoned him. The part of us which was him scattered away in ebbing sparks."

Div could feel the mourning . . .

The engines surged higher and a blaze of warmth rippled through the hull; he seemed to grow. Fleeting memories of flight, of power pirouettes performed in timeless reaches, mocking the stars in their stately unquestioning dance, flashed through his mind and drove the sadness back.

"There will be rejoicing when we return," said the ship-being. "No doubt we have been given up for lost, long since."

"But the *Pegasus*—what will become of it?"

"Dear love," said the ship-being. "How much indeed there is to learn just about yourself if you do not know *that*. For, after all, it is you who are responsible for the *Pegasus* following. As for what will become of it—that is a decision that you have already made."

TEN

Leana Coffer's Journal
(Vocoder transcription authorized
by Leana Coffer. Original recording
voice-locked per program 774-D.)

I had a troubling experience just now. I must try to get it down fresh, to remember it all as best I can, because it's forced me to a decision I may someday have great need to justify.

Last evening after my duty shift on the bridge, I lifted up to the deck three lounge for a drink. It's a relaxing place, when my thoughts will let me relax at all. At a corner booth at the far end of the lounge, I saw Lieutenant Norlan sitting with a man who seemed familiar though I couldn't place him. He was a Crysorian. When Norlan saw me, he motioned for me to join them and I did so because I was curious.

"Commander, this is Damilandor," Norlan said as I sat down. "He's spokesman for the Shector colonial expedition." I remembered the man then. I hadn't seen him since we'd picked up his expedition on Crysor many months ago.

"I'm pleased to meet you, Damilandor," I said.

"Please—Damil," he offered. "I am pleased also, and hopeful, to meet such an important person."

The waiter rolled up and I punched for a scotch and soda. I think Norlan ordered beer. Damil was still working his way through a concoction I didn't recognize—his fifth, in fact. If he was drunk I couldn't tell it. His eyes were hidden behind dark, cover-all contact lenses. No doubt he wore them for protection from the bright, Earth-normal ship lights.

"Damil here is counseling mutiny," Norlan said. He spoke flippantly, but I sensed tension in his voice—as if he were trying to gauge my reaction. Could I be trusted?

"He is joking," Damil interrupted hastily. "I am merely asking his assistance in putting a grievance before your captain."

"What sort of grievance?" I asked, pointedly ignoring Norlan's introductory remark. It was best to remain aloof, prepared to jump in whatever direction seemed safest after hearing Damil out.

"You see, Captain Darsen has violated the contract my people have signed with your service. We were promised delivery to Shector, which lies along your planned route of travel. But your captain has now changed that plan, and we must object. This is made difficult, however, because under that contract all my people are in your sleeper deck. As spokesman, I alone have been allowed to remain awake—and I am alone among strangers. Who will support my protest?"

I tried to explain that civilian passage agreements are always subject to changes in a ship's mission status. If Galactic Command had ordered us to pursue *Tin Woodman*, Darsen had no choice but to comply.

"You must both pardon me if I, not being part of your service, see the evidence differently," Damil said. "It does not add up, the way you say.

"It has been announced that the *Pegasus* is traveling on this jump five hundred light-years toward the galactic center. When all of Triunion-controlled space is less than *half* that distance in diameter, would your Galactic Command approve such a mission? And this—flight plan, do you say?—this flight plan has just been decided, after your captain has picked the mind of your shiplady for information. Would your Galactic Command have approved this journey in advance, when you had no way of knowing where the *Tin Woodman* had gone? I do not think so."

The remark about Mora particularly disturbed me. Norlan shook his head when I glared at him, indicating that he hadn't told Damil about the mind-pick. Who had, then? Damil must have been talking to other officers as well. This was dangerous—he was too outspoken to be safe aboard the *Pegasus*.

Damil plunged on, his voice rising, heedless of the lounge's other occupants. "I think your captain has taken it upon himself to order this mission. This is unlawful, it is a violation of our contract, and you must help me to make him turn back!"

I stood abruptly, which startled Norlan—he must have thought that I intended to arrest them both on the spot. What I really wanted was to get us all out of that lounge, to a place where no one could overhear Damil. I suggested that we go to the observation deck. No one is ever up there.

We lifted up to the observation deck, which seemed a familiar place to Damilandor. He said that he came here often and was amazed that the crew didn't seem to like the place.

"It's the service—and the ship itself," Norlan said. "So big we forget that it's not a world. So fragile, I guess, that we're afraid to think about what's beyond it."

Damil nodded. He seemed upset, confused that we had not answered his plea for help; but he continued talking about other subjects. He said that we seemed too attached to our machinery . . . that when we weren't working we tried to do as people on our home world might at leisure but that we didn't seem to get much pleasure from it. He thought that perhaps this was because we expected something more from the service.

About some things he was very wrongheaded, but mainly he was right.

I liked him, though some of what he said cut deep, and I cautioned him against speaking out too quickly in public while aboard the ship. He seemed to understand this.

"Finally leaving Crysor, bound for our new home, I suppose I forgot all my old cautions. But until we reach Shector, the Triunion rules still apply —I thank you for reminding me."

"Damil," I said, "why did your group apply for colonization rights?"

"Because we are Christians," he said.

That explained much. There's no officially sanctioned persecution of religious minorities on Crysor, of course, any more than there is on Earth. But I know what kind of danger the governments on Crysor see in beliefs like Damil's. They fear absorption by Earth's culture. For posterity's sake (and perhaps the record's as well) I should outline how I understand this situation to be:

About one hundred years before the first contact between Earth and Crysor, several Crysorian scientists came independently to the conclusion that they were not indigenous as a species to their world. Evidence of archaeology, zoology, and biochemistry seemed to point to this fact. The doctrine which these researchers promulgated under the name of colonization remade Crysorian society and thought as greatly as did *our* acceptance of evolutionary doctrine—but in a different direction. For if the human race had been *planted* on Crysor, then surely the planting must have been purposeful. Surely the Crysorians were part of a plan, the intent of which no one could guess. Further, no single group could credibly claim revealed or exclusive knowledge of such an unhuman plan for the human race's destiny—which did not mean that many had not tried.

Eventually, several of Crysor's industrialized nations had built powerful transmitting stations which beamed messages out into space. They did so, confident in their belief that someone was watching, listening. They believed that they would find their creators at last.

Instead, they had found Earth.

Earth: a human population of billions, almost half of which was engaged in one interminable war or another; a small part of the race beginning to claw its way out into space. The Crysorians were a more temperate people than Terrans; Earth seemed a slightly mad planet to them. As the two worlds exchanged information, any doubt that the Terran human race was ancestral to the Crysorian breed was removed. Likewise any suggestion that the Terrans themselves had been responsible for the transplant was shown as ludicrous. The Crysorian gods remained unrevealed, their existence more certain than ever, their nature still unknown.

The Crysorians were willing to accept Terrans as distant blood kin and as equals—but only that.

So when native Crysorians, subscribing to an ancient Terran religion in an archaic form, insisted that a Terran peasant's claim to intercession between humankind and the Creator extended to cover the Crysorians—well, the reaction of most Crysorians was hostile. It didn't help that the Christians implied that Christ had appeared on Earth because that planet was the true home of humanity—and therefore exalted above all other worlds.

The idea was intolerable, and so bred intolerance. I'm sure that the Crysorian governments were as happy to see Damilandor's people go as the Christians were happy to be leaving.

Damilandor never turned the conversation back again to his problem. He talked for a long time about his family, his people's plans for Shector, and I could see how lonely he had been aboard the *Pegasus*.

I was lonely, too. Damilandor saw too clearly the miserable reality of life aboard this ship, which I'd tried so long to deny. I've told myself that my resentment, my disenchantment with this place is due entirely to Darsen —but it isn't. The service itself is a failure, and I've failed by giving in to it.

So that is what happened last evening, as well as I remember it. That's what Damilandor said, and what I felt.

Just an hour ago, I learned that Darsen has arrested Damilandor, charging him with inciting to mutiny. Norlan told me this; he accused me of turning Damil in. I think I convinced Gary that he's wrong—I hope so. Have I been *that* aloof, or cold, or unfeeling?

Well . . . I did let them Dope Mora. I could have stopped that. God forgive me for that, for ever letting Darsen regain power on this ship. Because of that, Damil will never see Shector—I'm sure of it. How far does a person have to flee in this galaxy to be free?

The answer is to stop fleeing. Darsen was absolutely justified in arresting Damilandor—Damil is a greater threat to Darsen than either of them realizes. Because anyone who will think for himself, who will say what he thinks, is dangerous to Edan Darsen.

I won't stand for Darsen's abuses any longer.

I'll take this ship away from him.

There could be no doubt. Her Talent was returning.

In those long, slow days that followed the Null-R jump in pursuit of *Tin Woodman* it did not flow back suddenly, or with any marked effects—no sudden rush, no tumultuous wave of new sensations.

It came slowly, gently—like a lost cat returning to its master on silent, hesitant paws. And, curiously, she welcomed it. For all the pain it had bestowed upon her in the span of her life, she was used to it; it was a part of her total self, and though its absence was a relief from the constant pulsing of emotions from Normals, she realized that she had accustomed herself to that pain. Without the Talent, she seemed strangely out of contact with herself, as though she lacked some vital element of her nature.

For a time, this unusual man, this Ston Maurtan she had taken into her quarters, was an enigma to her. Had she her full faculties, perhaps the mysteries that permeated him, that looked bemusedly out of his brown, trusting eyes would be accessible to her understanding. Comprehension came gradually, like the full restoration of her Talent.

She grew to love him.

Mora presumed that Darsen knew she'd taken Ston under her wing. And there was no sign of the captain's disapproval or approval of this arrangement. Perhaps it was all the same to him; Ston would be equally out of the way in a Henderson, or under Mora's care. Maybe he was simply too preoccupied even to inquire as to the former ensign's present moneyless status; certainly Mora saw no sign either of him or his detestable henchman, Tamner, in that quiet, tense time following the successful discovery of the direction and destination of the alien. The two seemed to Mora to fade into ominous shadows; invisible presences whose control was all pervasive—a new and palpable aspect of the *Pegasus'* atmosphere.

But even though there was no further harassment of civilian Ston Maurtan, the malediction Captain Darsen had visited upon the man was still having its effects, its implications sinking deeper into him every day.

As Mora had also been relieved of her duties (without, as far as she could see, detriment to the crew's mental health), they were able to spend a good deal of time together. Only access to the control areas of the *Pegasus* was denied them; the rest of the ship was at their disposal. The extent and variety of this was not inconsiderable; the *Pegasus* was equipped with almost every legal diversion available to modern man. They spent this free time liberally sampling all the entertainments of this little, movable world. They strolled through the hydroponic gardens, breathing in the heavy, hot, flower-perfumed air. They frequented the Tri-Vid parlors, the feelies, the game rooms, the Null-G room, the skating rink, the concert hall.

It was all very peaceful and relaxing to Mora after the incident-filled preceding days. Nevertheless, there was the nagging feeling at the back of her mind that all this was just a lull in the drama, the eye of the whirlwind. The end of the pursuit loomed in the future; Mora tried not to think about it. Certainly, she told herself, the chase was stupid, hopeless. Its fruitlessness would soon dawn upon Captain Darsen, and they would return. But another part of her was reserved for the constant fear that she had betrayed Div; that the *Pegasus* and its captain intended nothing good for *Tin Woodman* should they, by some freak circumstance, overtake it. But she kept all these fears and self-doubts safely imprisoned in a corner of her mind.

She immersed herself in the amusements available on the ship. She immersed herself in Ston.

It was strange.

Because most of her time was spent with him, her attention fixed upon his moods, his feelings, the gradual stepping-up of her Talent, the revelatory flashes of its increased power, occurred while focused on Ston. These surprised her, and she welcomed them for the understanding they gave of this man she cared for. But what astonished her most was that sometimes she felt these abrupt, unsettling dives into his emotions while he was nowhere near. As though she were gradually tuning into the unique personality frequency that was Ston Maurtan.

And as though he were tuning, somehow, into hers.

Certainly, Ston welcomed the deepening of their relationship. During their days together, she could see the signs on all levels: he was coming to depend on her. And because of her burgeoning Talent, she could perceive that this dependence was a tumbling into past days for Ston, a renewing of a past relationship, substituting Mora for his sister Adria. It pleased her to be helping him so; he was loose and free and trusting about her; it was very clear that he was loving her from the depths of his being. But at the same time was it the sort of love that she wanted from this man? And was it really for her, and not some resurrected spirit of this Adria Maurtan that Ston seemed to detect in her?

Or maybe he was merely using his past relationship with his sister as a model—and was afraid to take it any further. He seemed to balk at the notion of venturing too far into a physical expression of love with her. Mora understood this and bided her time, not trying to hurry anything. But often it frustrated her.

After all, she thought, waving her hand over the door mechanism of her cabin. *I'm* not Adria. *I'm* not!

"Hoo boy!" whooshed Ston, collapsing into a cross-legged position on his crumpled bedclothes. He peered up at her with playful but weary eyes. "That Null-G room takes a lot out of you."

She poured two cups of guava juice, handed him one. "It does if you play grav-ball like a lunatic. If you didn't have those protective pads, you'd have killed yourself, bouncing off those walls like you did."

"But, Mora, that's part of the *fun*," he declared after thirstily downing over half the drink. "That's what sports are for—to pound one's violent tendencies out, relieving tensions."

"Do you think they'd have let you play if they knew who you were?"

He looked up, confused. "Hey. What's that supposed to mean?"

"I mean, the only reason you could relieve your tensions with them is that they didn't realize you were Ston Maurtan."

"Maybe. Maybe not. I admit, I didn't know them from my previous duties." After tossing down the last of the drink, he handed the cup back to her. "How come the reminder? You think I don't realize what you've been doing for me? You think I don't appreciate it? You know, come to think of it, you've been kind of moody all evening. You haven't actually acted moody—but I can sort of sense it. It's funny, Mora, but I haven't had that sensation with anybody since—"

"Since Adria," she finished for him quietly, putting the cups away. As soon as she'd said it, she wished she hadn't. There was a long pause from him. She was afraid to turn around and look at him. Afraid even to reach out tentatively with her Talent and take the pulse of his feelings. Sometimes words said in the wrong way could be very cruel.

"Yes," he said finally. "Not since Adria, Mora. That's quite true. Adria was kind, and loving, and generous. Just like you. Only you're almost better. You're not my sister."

Spinning about, she looked at him in disbelief. "Aren't I?" Black clouds of unreasoning anger were forming in her mind.

Ston recoiled as if struck. "What . . . ? What did I say?"

She advanced on him, fuming. "What's my name, Ston? *What's my name?*" she almost screamed at him.

"Mora. Mora Elbrun, of course." The hurt look in his eyes took a little of the frustrated fury out of her. But not all.

"Are you sure it's not *Adria*, like you keep on wanting to call me? Not Addy? You might as well call me that, Ston, because that's who I am to you." She turned away.

There was a long silence from Ston. Then she heard him rise and felt him touch her arm. "I'm sorry," he said. "Let's not talk about Adria, any more. Maybe you have become like a sister to me, though. Maybe I love you like a sister. But what's wrong with that? What's wrong with love?"

She walked away, sat in a chair, looked at him. "Nothing, Ston, if your love is for a person, and not a memory you see being relived in that person."

"Where's your brandy, Mora?" he asked quietly.

"I thought you didn't drink."

"Medicinal purposes. I won't get drunk. Just a glass."

"My cabinet."

"Thanks."

She closed her eyes, listening to the clunking noises, the splash of liquid. There was a long silence. It had all come out so suddenly . . .

"Mora." She realized he was standing over her. She opened her eyes, and he sat down beside her, a glass of amber liquid in his hand. "Mora, I apologize for what I've been doing. But it's very hard . . . very hard not to confuse you with Adria sometimes. Maybe I'm just hurting both of us. I don't know. But I've been thinking. We know we care about one another, and we've had a great time. But we're living in a dream—we have to face reality. I've been meaning to talk to you about it; I might as well do that now. There's really no reason for you to be spending money, when Darsen is obviously perfectly willing to put me in a Henderson until we return to our next port of call. That way we can save your money, use it wherever we end up. Besides, I feel like a burden to you."

"I owe it to you, Ston," she replied.

"You don't owe me anything, really. That whole escape business was entirely *worthless*. You would not have been given any more treatments, whatever happened. I just complicated things a bit."

"But you didn't *know* that. You tried, and that's what's important, Ston. You did what you thought was right. Your feelings for me came only after the fact. It was your principles that made you do it."

"And the fact that you hit something in me first time I saw you. Something that reminded me of Adria. The whole setup. Reminded me of what happened to Adria." He sighed and sipped his brandy. "And maybe, I keep on telling myself, if I'd been there to help instead of off earning my stars in the service, she'd have been able to hang on. To beat them. But no. I was light-years away. So far. So very far away when the pressure got too much for her."

"What was it, Ston?"

"A man." He laughed, humorlessly. "Pretty simple, huh? Well, as near as I could get it, that was just the final straw. Bad luck seemed to vortex on her, and that was it—a guy broke her heart. And guess what, Mora. This is the funniest part. The bastard was in the Triunion Space Service. You think maybe she substituted him for me? Isn't that a chuckle?" He stared at the wall, bleakly. "Isn't that the funniest thing you ever heard in your life?"

"Ston," she said in a whisper. "I want you to love *me*—not a memory. She's dead. You have to accept that. I'm not her."

"Doesn't make any difference now." He gulped down the rest of the brandy. "I think I'd better request placement in a Henderson. I think that's best for both of us—the most practical thing. Just for the duration of the trip—when we get back to Earth, or wherever, we'll get something together. God knows what, but we'll manage." He patted her hand. "It's been great—you've improved my whole pessimistic outlook."

"We might never get back to Earth, Ston."

He cocked his head quizzically.

"We're far away from Triunion space now. On a crazy chase with a question mark at its end. Darsen's flipped out for some reason. I don't know if the *Pegasus* will ever return. It's a definite possibility—and I don't like the thought of spending these days alone. They might be my last. I can spare the money."

He nodded. "What if I said my pride wouldn't allow that."

"Then I'd tell you what you can do with your stupid pride."

He laughed, unguardedly and fully. A rich laugh, full of love. "You know, that's just what . . ." He stopped himself, laughed again, and hugged her.

Just what Adria would have said, she finished the sentence for him in her mind. But she felt no anger.

She could wait until he was ready.

Leana Coffer's Journal
(Vocoder transcription authorized
by Leana Coffer. Original recording
voice-locked per program 774-D.)

Keeping this journal is becoming dangerous. I should stop, but somehow I feel the need to justify myself day by day—if only to myself.

I'm not sure that I'm being watched, but it's likely. Someone must have reported seeing Norlan and me with Damilandor in the lounge. It's equally certain that this incident was not the one which caused Damil's arrest, otherwise Norlan and I would be in the brig too. As matters stand, I must continue to be the efficient, unfeeling executive officer that I've always been—ignoring even the slight to my position in Darsen's appointment of Tamner as his personal assistant. Darsen has turned almost all of his regular duties over to Tamner, as though the captain's full attention is needed for our pursuit of the alien. Tamner is now effectively second in command, with more power than me.

Five days have passed since we went into Null-R. This ship is now traveling through the Null-R continuum at the maximum velocity the engines can achieve, and the chief engineer complains constantly that it is dangerous for us to keep up this speed for long periods of time. Now and then, Darsen gives in for a while. But after a few hours he demands acceleration again.

He sits behind his command desk all his waking hours—and is sleeping only four hours out of every twenty-four. He has his meals brought to him at his desk.

Unrest among the crew has become so great that six people, including one of the bridge crew, have been confined to MedSec for "psychiatric observation." In the lower echelons, where personality monitoring is less closely maintained, morale is even worse. This is not an exploratory vessel, and the crew is not emotionally prepared for this sort of crazy chase. No one is happy about Darsen's mission. The most excitable of the crew members complain openly, and too loudly for their own good.

To top this all off, we have a food shortage now—we were to have stopped over for supplies long ago, on our regular run. So what does Tamner—damn him—suggest? Well, there's an obscure regulation which covers this situation—members of the crew may be placed into Hendersons for the duration of the shortage. Same applies to passengers. And there's no doubt that the first selected for this will be the complainers and potential troublemakers.

For the moment I'll have to let the loudmouths draw attention so that less will land on me. And I must use this borrowed time to plan.

Darsen must be taking stimulants in great dosage; I'm tempted to think that if I give him time he'll simply collapse or go obviously berserk—but I can't depend on that. That his unbalance is so visible, however, is to my advantage.

The captain obviously obsessed, the crew anxious and unhappy; the mutiny *must* succeed, given the circumstances. My problem has been one of contacting and organizing the people I need with me. I must be furtive about this, and able to trust them completely—until now this has stumped me. But I've thought of a way to do it, a way which demands that I risk approaching and trusting absolutely only one person.

I need Mora Elbrun.

ELEVEN

She stood on a craggy cliff, overlooking the sea.

Below, waves beat themselves thunderously to froth against sharp, black rocks. She could smell their briny spume, borne aloft on the wind that white-capped the waves and pushed a solitary gull up toward the blue, cumulus-spotted sky. The salty tang dominated the air, but the clean, rich tastes of the grass and the forest, and perhaps even the heather that clothed the sides of the rough mountains humping along the horizon, were there as well.

Beside her, in tartan plaids, stood Ston Maurtan, smiling, looking off as though through a great distance.

"It's very beautiful here," she told him. "Just on the brow of that hill there's a crumbling castle. There's a sea gull just drifting in the breeze. He looks content, Ston. Too bad we can't just be gulls, swooping and playing above a Scottish sea."

"Yeah," Ston replied absently.

"You know," she said crossly, "you *could* have selected the same program as I did. I think you just took the Grand Canyon to be obstinate."

He turned to face her. "I can't stand the goddamned seashore of Scotland. Never could. Really much more scenic here. More relaxing. The air is dry and clean. The sun is hot, but pleasant." He looked at her, smiling. His eyes were hidden behind goggles, but she was sure they had a gleam to them from the emotions she could feel in them. "And we're both in cowboy suits."

"Cowboy suits!" she cried, in a mock-horrified voice.

"Yeah, with ten-gallon hats, and fringes, and everything. Boots included."

"Oh, my god!" She laughed. "That's disgusting."

"Well, I bet you've got us in tartan, haven't you."

"It's part of the program. I could have fitted you out in a kilt and bagpipes, if I wanted. But my selection has *taste*."

She couldn't help but chuckle. She slipped her hand in his and squeezed. It would have been nice to tiptoe up and kiss him—but that would have been awkward with the complicated set of attachments in masklike array on both their faces, with the web of wires connected to the backpack computer-terminal extension. So she contented herself with holding his hand.

God, it was romantic! The sea, the land, the castle, all harmonizing into a symphony of the senses. Her Talent was focused on Ston to such a degree that she was only aware of his presence, successfully shutting out the other extrasensory data available from the reality of the ship's Garden Room, where they actually stood. The rental of the Otherwhere devices and the computer time was expensive. But it was worth it to be swept away from the grim metal of the *Pegasus* into an Ideal. Here, it was easy to pretend that she was a Scots lass beside her handsome highwayman lover who was about to carry her off into the heather for mutual ravishment.

A mental fantasy to match the physical one around her. Looking at Ston, she laughed to herself, feeling like an adolescent. The relationship between herself and Ston was a bit too delicate for that sort of thing to happen yet. He still had to straighten himself out on that score.

Standing there now with him in her private computer-structured fantasy, she wished he would hurry up about it.

Her gaze swept the panorama again. Behind them crew people were milling about, reclothed to her sight in suitably Scottish apparel. A solitary woman dressed in a smart knee-length kilt was heading their way, evidently intent on speaking with them.

She tapped Ston's shoulder. "Someone's coming. A woman."

"Can't see her. I've got everybody but you programmed out."

"You'd better tune her in, then. I think I recognize her . . . yes, it's Leana Coffer!"

Reaching down to the abdomen attachment, Ston fiddled with a dial. "Damn it, I'm losing the canyon now too. Oh. There. Yeah. I see her."

Leana Coffer stopped in front of them. "Hello, Mora. Can you hear me?"

Instantly, Mora directed her Talent toward the woman and took a surface reading. Concern. Sincerity.

"She's speaking, isn't she?" said Ston, adjusting his computer-interface controls. "All I can hear is you, the wind, and some burro honking in the distance."

"Yes," Mora replied to the new arrival. "I can hear you, anyway. I'm sure Ston will tune you in eventually."

Coffer nodded. "I was just walking through the Garden Room, and I saw you two. I just wanted to see how you are doing. By the way, what are you tuned into on those devices?"

"Scottish coast," Mora answered hesitantly. Generally, everyone simply ignored them. Why had Coffer approached, in a friendly manner yet? "Ston's in the Grand Canyon."

"Hell, I can't tune her in!" cried Ston. "What's wrong with this stinking machine? We paid good money . . ."

Disregarding Ston, Mora said to Coffer, somewhat bitterly: "You should know I'm no longer shiplady, Leana. If you have problems . . ."

The woman waved her hands in negation. "Oh no. Nothing like that. Listen, Mora—actually, I want to apologize. But you have to understand, I had no choice but to do what I did . . . to carry out Darsen's orders. Shall we put it all behind us?"

Mora shrugged, reached down, and hit the cutoff button. The sea, the sky, the cliff, the distant mountains dissolved into the trees, the ceiling, the flowers and surrounding plants of the large, square Garden Room. Coffer's kilt vanished, giving way to the maroon and tan of command crew leisure attire. Ston still played with his knobs, without success.

"Your entire interface with the computer has been disengaged?" inquired Coffer, glancing about as though to make sure no one watched.

"Yes. Why?"

"Good. As far as I know there is no security surveillance to speak of in this area. But I can't be positive. So I'll be brief. Please appear to be chatting casually with me." She took a breath. "Things are getting bad. I think you might be able to help. We can't risk speaking at length here. There is to be a dance tonight, in the amphitheater. There will be privacy booths available, and minimal surveillance. Meet me there, both of you, and I'll explain everything."

"How do I know this isn't one of Darsen's little traps?" Mora asked suspiciously.

"Your Talent should be back now. I'm not hiding anything. By all means read me. But quickly. I've got to go. I'll reserve the table. In the back. I'll be there. It's at 2000 hours."

Even as Coffer spoke, Mora was already letting herself penetrate Coffer's emotions further. There was no sign of deceit there; from all indications, she was being entirely truthful. Not merely that—under her relaxed exterior, she was wound up tight as a spring. She was frightened. She did not attempt to erect any barriers against Mora. The invitation was obvious; Mora would be allowed to probe even further, if she wanted.

But it was enough. She trusted Coffer now.

"We'll be there. But will it be risky?"

"Yes," Coffer replied.

"But why can't we talk in my quarters?"

"Bugged, I'm sure."

She nodded. Damn them. Listening in on her and Ston . . .

"All right. So nice to see you again, Leana. Thanks for your concern." She gave Coffer a pleasant smile.

Coffer returned it and continued in the direction she'd been heading when she had "bumped" into them, merely strolling along, enjoying the flora.

"There," said Ston, looking up. "Where did Coffer go? And what did she want?"

Mora grabbed him by the crook of his arm. "We're turning these contraptions in, Ston. I'll explain." She tugged him quickly around a corner. He yelped, covering his eyes. "Don't—you're pulling me over the side . . ."

Halting abruptly, they looked at each other and broke into laughter.

It was his big mouth that got Engineer Third Class Monte Thompson into trouble. The feisty, one-point-seven-meter Null-R Field Generator Inspector from Sicily certainly never entertained thoughts of actually going against *any* officers, let alone the captain, no matter if they were headed into the Inner Circle of Dante's Inferno itself. But he complained loudly and openly, underlining his protestations against the ship's course with violent, barely controlled gestures. Security was certainly cognizant of the man, particularly because of his potentially harmful proximity to highly important mechanisms. The incident in the mess hall, however, decided them on what they should do about him.

Climbing up and down the web-working that surrounded the stasis engines, checking for mechanical faults or signs of wear in the huge machines in the port bow of the *Pegasus* tended to be exhausting work at best. But ten days' straight long-shift duty was really wearing him out. His loud grumblings about the extra work and dubious destination were actually only his way of letting off steam. He liked the job. He liked his pay. He enjoyed being a part of this little universe inside the ship; so much better than back on Earth. He felt important here. Significant. It was much better to be a small anchovy in a small pond, than a small anchovy in an ocean. Crawling about in the webbing, adjusting this and that, checking meters—the thought never occurred to him that the monitor attachment to the computer from the engines did most of his actual work—was tiring. Usually when he was done with a shift, he was ravenous.

He expected a decent amount of food supplied him to restore expended energy.

So when Chief Petty Officer Wilmo told him his tour of duty was over, he cried, "About goddamn time," jumped down lithely from the strong nylon web, and headed straight for some chow. Although not as good as the stuff he ate at home, the food here wasn't bad. It was filling, and fairly tasty. A combination of soybean hydroponics, cultivated algae, and some synthesis of nutrient from inorganic chemicals, often spiced with specials from the growing rooms, it was somehow formed into palatable, varied meals. Not the real thing of course. And it took a while to get used to the idea that some of it was recycled wastes, but then when you got down to it, Earth wasn't a hell of a lot better, really. As his sinewy, diminutive form made its way to Mess Hall Three, his mind was adding sensuous detail to the savory image of the dinner he was going to punch up. Steak. Gravy. A side dish of buttered spaghetti with a sprinkling of oregano and Romano cheese. Yeah. And some eggplant! Cooked in olive oil, simmered with tomato sauce, topped with mozzarella. And to drink: a nice glass of wine. A little over regular rations, sure. But he could cough up an extra expense unit. And a salad! Don't forget the salad!

It would be worth it.

Entering the nearly empty mess an hour before his usual dinnertime, he had to swallow the saliva that had gushed into his mouth. Damn! He could almost smell it, and the computer hadn't even put it together yet!

Eagerly, he bounced over to the Special Dinner section, slipped in his identicard, pondered the dials. After the necessary manipulations, he keypunched the specific directions: STEAK, EGGPLANT, SPAGHETTI AL DENTE, YOU LOUSY CHEF MACHINE—OIL AND VINEGAR ON THE SALAD—AND DON'T COOK THE HELL OUT OF THE STEAK THIS TIME, HUH? RARE. RARE!

He ordered his wine, fingered the final control, and the machine came to life. Three minutes later—a little fast, he noticed—it dinged its completion, and he slid open the little door expectantly. He pulled out the tray.

There, on a single dish, was a pale gray patty of unornamented soy meat, a little puddle of algae-veg, and a glass of soy milk.

He put the tray down on the table, pounded on the console keys. YOU MADE A MISTAKE. WHAT THE SHIT IS WRONG WITH YOU? I ORDERED—

The keys became stiff. The screen responded: BECAUSE OF SUPPLY PROBLEMS, CAPTAIN DARSEN HAS ORDERED SPECIAL RATIONING. PLEASE BEAR WITH US DURING THIS EMERGENCY.

He blew up.

He headed straight for an intra-ship communicator.

"Bridge Communications."

After telling the bridge what it could do with itself, he demanded to speak to the captain. When bridge communications told him that the captain was unavailable and coldly asked him what the problem was, he told them. "What is this rationing shit? I got a tray full of dreck down here! You expect me to *eat* this? Listen—I just worked a backbreaking six goddamn hours on the frigging engines, and I want something to *eat!* If this is the sort of treatment we can expect on this harebrained trip light-years away from our intended course, I say we turn back!"

The other people in the mess, looking up from equally slim rations, added their cheers of approval.

"Just a moment, Mr. Thompson," the voice comforted. "We'll send someone down immediately to attend to the problem."

When the security force got there and asked him politely to come with them to speak with Lieutenant Commander Tamner, Thompson threw the food at them. The security men suddenly found themselves being showered with the other trays of food in the hall. After a small fracas, they managed to administer a quick stun to the rabble-rouser and carted him away bodily. The others were also subdued.

Tamner had Hendersons all ready for them.

They entered the amphitheater at 2013 hours. The dance was already in full swing.

There was no question in Mora's mind why the dance had been scheduled. It was a proven fact that dancing—particularly the sort of frenzied dancing that was allowed in the large amphitheater—relieved tension. No doubt the new security chief, Jin Tamner, detected the tension that was building in the crew members and passengers as they speeded further and further away from known space, and wished to bleed it off the safest way possible.

She wore a streamlined jumpsuit, emblazoned with colored glitter. Ston was dressed in a simple coverall.

The center of the amphitheater had been cleared of seats for the "dance floor." The walls, floor, and ceiling of the huge room were literally one entire sound system, augmented for this event by separate sonic boxes in the corners for special aural effects reserved for concerts and dances.

As they entered, she was immediately buffeted by the blast of sound that swelled around her from every direction. She could not merely hear the music—now a simple rhythmic composition, cleverly underpinned with a complex, entirely separate melody that counterpointed the basic dance song—she could feel it over every square centimeter of her body. The sound was that penetrating. It coursed over her like a strong current of warm friendly water, buoying up her spirits with the emotion it imparted.

The darkened room was strobed with delicate light-interpretations of the music. Varied pulses and scintillations and dazzles splashed over the ceiling, ribbed with lasers. Colors throbbed. The blisters on the floor and wall that were the light machines fairly blazed like confused suns, now merely throwing off subtle flares of spectruming flashes, now exploding into fountains of resplendence. All flashed perfect visions of the tone and beat of the music to where the sound would not go.

The music itself was created by a single man, sitting off in the corner of the stage, almost invisible beneath an array of equipment. On his head was a helmet with dozens of attached wires snaking off into machines. A music man, his brain surgically implanted with special jacks and electrical connections, he literally plugged himself into a computer which translated the music he had in his mind into the varied sounds heard by the dancers. Some songs he would compose on the spot; most he drew from memory, subtly shading them with appropriate emotion. The cumbersome interface of musical instruments was thus eliminated. It was one step further in direct musical communication.

The sounds the music man could make were breath-takingly, soul-achingly beautiful.

Totally involved, augmented by other sensual accouterments, one could visit a dance and be totally swept away on a wave of continuous ecstasy. Portable taste and olfactory attachments that complemented both the sound and the sights were available. The dance floor consisted of a circular, flat area centered with a large, ceiling-high free-fall field. Dancers could, at will, hurl themselves into this and gyrate free of ship's gravity.

Surrounding the dance floor were tables. By the spurious light, Mora searched out Leana Coffer . . . and found her, sitting near the back, alone.

Mora tugged Ston's sleeve, pointed toward Coffer's table. Ston seemed to be startled out of temporary immersion in the music—he nodded and, holding hands, they threaded through the tables and chairs.

Coffer waved hello and urged them to sit down. As they did so, she tapped the privacy field over the table, shutting out all the sound.

"Hey," complained Ston. "Do you have to do that? I was enjoying the music."

"The dance lasts till at least midnight. This won't take too long. Sound coming in means that sound can go out as well. I don't want that."

Ston shrugged and sighed. "Okay. What's up?"

Pushing forward two filled glasses, Coffer said, "I got you beer. That okay?"

"Sure." Mora accepted hers, sipped. "A bit weak."

"Watered down. The rationing effective this afternoon."

"Yes. Dinner was dreadful," she said.

"It's bringing a lot of the unrest on board to the surface," said Coffer. "It might help our cause to a degree. For example, today a guy from Engineering *really* got bent out of sorts. I hear he threw his dinner right into Tamner's face—but that's only scuttlebutt, and you know how that's distorted." Her expression grew grim. "But I do know that he's raised his complaints before, and Tamner 'arbitrarily' selected him and a few others involved in that minor riot to be placed in Hendersons for the duration of the 'emergency' to alleviate the food supply shortage."

"And to effectively eliminate troublemakers," put in Ston.

"Yes. I'm afraid that appears to be the ploy." Coffer swallowed some beer, made a face.

"Okay, Leana," said Mora. "Here we are, risking placement in Hendersons as well. Specifically, why did you want to talk to Ston and me?"

The woman sucked in breath, let it out contemplatively. "Things are very bad upstairs. We're headed God-knows-where on a fool's mission. Captain Darsen's gone off the deep end. The course of action was *not* ordered by Galactic Command—I'm sure of that. And Tamner's become a little dictator. Very bad." She paused, staring away.

Crimson light streaked with white dots spilled across the table like a ghost of burning lava. Mora could almost feel the floor and the force screen vibrating with the thunderous music dashing itself against them, trying to get in, drown the party in sound.

"Are you suggesting mutiny, Leana?"

The executive officer looked into Mora's eyes and nodded slowly.

TWELVE

Leana Coffer's Journal
(Vocoder transcription authorized
by Leana Coffer. Original recording
voice-locked per program 774-D.)

I feel giddy, elated. Perhaps I'm a little drunk—certainly a novel sensation. I should have restrained myself at the dance where I talked with Mora and her friend . . . so much depends now on my being in complete control. Yet I've never been less afraid, more certain of success, than now. Perhaps . . . I remember my mother as a terrible drinker. Father pretended it didn't bother him. He used to call it her "courage." It made her so courageous that she killed them both in a traffic accident when I was thirteen . . . but I don't want to think about that . . .

Learning that the exec had a mother would probably shock the crew worse than anything else in this journal.

I hadn't seen Mora since the *Tin Woodman* incident. I think I've gained her trust—and I think she's worried that maybe Darsen will find *Tin Woodman* and Div again, and do them harm. So mutiny is just fine with her. Seeing Mora tonight, I remembered the dedication with which she used to ply her so ineffectual trade. The role of shiplady, like so many service assignments and regulations, has always seemed an illogical one. In a universe top-heavy with psychologists, why are Talents needed on starships? There must be a reason for this foolishness—and tonight I've put it all together. Call it Coffer's manifesto—the *raison d'être* of the mutiny. Or is it a revolution? We're all alone, out here on the ship; it's the only world we have. Call it revolution, then.

The Triunion Space Service is a drain which keeps society stable. It's a dream that every youngster has, to be a spacer and drift from star to star, or venture boldly out to find new worlds. Well, then, let them. They won't be at home, making trouble.

There are over five hundred crew people aboard the *Pegasus*, too many of them officers. And they do unnecessary things—this ship could be run by twenty people; the ship's computer does most of the work. However, if it were, how many ships would the service need to guarantee a place for representatives of every social, racial, national, and ideological group? We have a quota system operating here, I think.

Take Earth—dominated by six superstates so interdependent on one another that war is unthinkable. The threat to these governments is not each other, but the populations they each control. The service is set up as a shining example of courageous people expanding man's knowledge, building a better world out among the stars. Everyone wants to join it—the governments can thus get their rebels, boat-rockers, overachievers and other likely troublemakers to *volunteer* for the service. Then they send them out to push buttons on useless machinery light-years from home; a much better thing to do than to let them hang about the Triunion home-worlds starting revolutions.

The colonies fit into this scheme as well. They can't develop quickly enough ever to threaten or oppose the Triunion—and why should they want to? They've got their own worlds, all to themselves. This way, people who won't fit, don't qualify, or just represent too large a group to be in the Space Service can be disposed of. For example, Damilandor. Crysor didn't want him and his fellow Christians, and certainly couldn't expect them all to sign on for space duty. So they were offered a world of their own.

Now, as for the Talents; they're disliked and treated with suspicion by most of humanity. The worst fear expressed is that they'll coalesce into some sort of conspiratorial group. Most of them would never qualify for the service—they'd never pass the psych exams—unless there were a job that only they could do. Ergo, the shiplady/shipman position. One to a ship, and always under close supervision.

I'm only guessing at all this, but it has the ring of truth—to me, at least. Perhaps I'm just getting as paranoid as Darsen. But consider—the major aim of all government is self-perpetuation. In the service, the governments have found a means of avoiding disruptive change which might threaten their hegemonies. It's commonly observed that civilization on Earth has evolved very little since the late twentieth century, and I think my theory goes a long way to explaining why.

The service is a medieval solution to a modern problem; we're a leech on the body politic, draining the bad blood—and the good blood, as well.

I've been trying to sleep, without success. My conversation with Mora and Ston keeps replaying itself. I had meant to set down the outlines here of the plan I discussed with them—but my involvement with my own theories ran away with me. I shall do so now.

Mora's sympathy with my intentions was clear—she is as disenfranchised and suffers as greatly under Darsen as anyone. She has the ability to read emotions and therefore was easy to persuade as far as my own sincerity is concerned; for the same reason I'm willing to trust Ston Maurtan as long as she does.

Her Talent is central to my plan. I explained this to her—through brief nonverbal contact with others she can gauge their willingness to oppose Darsen. She can guarantee that we take no spies into our confidence; at the same time she can determine who among the many possible allies in each area of ship's operations will be the most valuable to us.

I explained briefly what I would expect out of each recruit. I told her that I had settled on a code-phrase to trigger action, which would be broadcast by Gary Norlan, who's already quite involved: "Compliments of the captain." This will begin the mutiny. She is to pass this phrase on to those she recruits. I think it's a good signal; it's ordinarily attached to some general order relaxing restrictions or declaring special recreation for the crew, and therefore isn't likely to be used in any regular broadcast from the bridge. Not while Darsen is in command.

Then the mutiny will begin.

They were almost there, now: the destination.

Tucked at the heart of *Tin Woodman* like a baby in its mother's womb, Div Harlthor was slowly learning who he had become, and who he had been before. More and more, in the wordless discussions between *Tin Woodman* and Div, he felt as though he were conversing with himself. But as hard as he tried he could not merge himself totally—there was an empty space in him, yet. He brooded much even as he learned to touch the vibrant energies of the universe, and to use them.

He thought about the people he had known. He thought often about Mora Elbrun. He needed to think as himself—not something more. He tried to withdraw his mind into the tiny part of the ship-being which was still totally separate—*his*.

"Why do you persist in keeping part of yourself removed, my love?" asked *Tin Woodman*, concerned.

"I don't know. I just have to."

"It is to be expected perhaps. It is not easy to cast oneself away from the things one has known all one's previous life. Perhaps we can discuss this?"

But Div could not explain. He was beginning to comprehend how utterly and irrevocably he had cut himself off from his past, from other human beings. Those thoughts and feelings which he had once desperately wished to share with some other person in the frustrated hope that they might be reciprocated welled up in him now. But he *had* an other, now, didn't he? And more love than he could imagine . . . yet maybe not the sort he had desired. . . .

Div tried to open himself and communicate this undefined feeling —and Mora Elbrun seemed on his mind once more.

It had seemed so wildly beyond his reach, on the *Pegasus*—the possibility of feeling something more than his familiar uncertain empathy for another person—a particular person. His feelings for her had been unexamined and undiscovered while his fascination and obsession with the mystery of *Tin Woodman* had grown. Now he regretted—

What had been his hopes and desires before all of this? He had those then—and ideals below the pain and the endurance. To fulfill himself? To discover the *reason* for his existence? At one time, in the worst part of his life—almost insane, when they had put him away— he believed in nothing. Life was absurd, without meaning, a freak smear of matter and energy gyrating mindlessly in the midst of measureless vacuum. He had wanted to die then—no, he even wished he had never existed. That was the lowest plunge, when he had tried to kill himself and they stopped him. And Dr. Severs had said, "Well, Div, if you find a key, you know there must be a lock somewhere." That phrase stood out long after the other things that Severs had said drifted away into his subconscious. Perhaps he *was* a key to something . . . perhaps he had a *purpose* in life, a place to *belong*. This was why he had assented to leaving Earth to contact the alien the *Pegasus* had found—somehow knowing that perhaps this would give his life meaning, if only in service to the human race in some obscure way. He had found much more, hadn't he? Here, with the universe at the finger tips of his mind, and a future of wonder awaiting him—didn't this surpass everything he had dreamed of before, yearned for achingly?

Yes, he told himself in his secret heart. Of course.

Of course. . . .

The kid in the mess hall would be number sixteen.

It was working.

Alone, she pulled her tray out of the service machine, turned around, and trained her eyes on her target. He was sitting in a desolate corner of the nearly empty room, forlornly forking his slim rations into his mouth. Couldn't be more than twenty-three, she figured. Face hardly touched by beard. Soft hazel eyes beneath auburn bangs. Ston had identified him. A spanking-new ensign, assigned to the *Pegasus* at the same time as Ston had been. Ensign Dinni Rosher. *A good guy to talk to,* Ston had said. *Always very moody, when I knew him. Very disappointed with the service. He should be a knockover, the way things are now.*

She made a point of passing behind him on her way to the food dispenser machine. The emotions that waved from him were fairly negative: unhappiness, tinged with real bitterness. Above all, he seemed terribly tired. She felt for him.

"Mind if I sit here?"

His head jerked up at her words. His eyes were startled. "Uh— why?"

"I'm lonely. It depresses me to sit alone in this place." Tentatively, she brushed his mind with a soft, comforting stroke of empathy.

"There are others around."

"But you're the only one by yourself."

"Oh." He smiled dutifully, nodded at the chair across from him. "Sure. Have a seat. I don't promise you fascinating company."

"Simple company will do."

"Yeah," he whispered. "Simple."

Mora set her tray down. "I didn't mean it that way."

"Don't mind me."

"You don't look too cheery. How come?" The tentative brush of her Talent undeflected, she allowed more empathy to wash over him, gradually. Already, she could feel him loosening up. Good. A susceptible mind.

"Oh," he said after sipping at his half-gone soy milk. "Things."

"Not so good?"

He looked up at her. "Are they good for anyone nowadays?"

"No. I suppose not."

He looked more closely at her. "Hey. I know who you are. The shiplady. Yeah. Mora. Mora—"

"Elbrun."

"Yes. I never used you."

"I'd remember you."

"Rumor is you started us on this crazy goose chase."

"Not really. I had no choice. It was the captain—who gave the orders. Not me."

"Galactic Command, you mean."

She probed. A very upset fellow, this Dinni Rosher. He fairly resonated dissatisfaction. It showed up as moroseness on the surface —but she could detect much more beneath. The emotions he gave off when voicing "captain" and "Galactic Command" were negative. Very negative indeed. He was ripe.

She sighed softly, rubbing her short length of yellow hair as she spoke. "I hear it was Captain Darsen who authorized pursuit of the alien. Not Galactic Command."

His hazel eyes stared straight into hers. "That's impossible."

"Suppose it was possible," she countered airily, playing with her food, making it all seem light and cheerful—a little game.

"Then the captain is—no . . . it's unthinkable." He shook his head conclusively.

Raising her fork, she waved at him slightly. "Well, suppose the captain *has* taken the matter in his own hands. Suppose he *disobeyed* Galactic Command, and for his own reasons took off after the alien. It does make sense, doesn't it? I mean, Galactic Command sending us off on a fool's mission, with low supplies—many, many light-years from known space. It's unprecedented. Would the usually conservative GC do such a thing when the odds are slim to none of catching the quarry? Which, you have to admit, can hardly be categorized as hostile to the Triunion. Suppose all this is the case."

"What are you getting at?" His food sat before him, forgotten.

Her smile stiffened. "Who is our actual allegiance to in the service? Our captain—or Galactic Command?"

He turned his eyes away, nodding. "Yes. I see what you mean. But what *proof* do you have? You've used the word 'suppose' a lot."

This was the most difficult part, because there was no solid tangible proof to give. Only Coffer's word. It was necessary at this point to convince him both with her rhetoric and her subtle manipulations of his emotions. She had never been very good at that as a shiplady. But in her present role she tried as hard as she could.

"No such order from Galactic Command was ever received."

"But how do you know that for a *fact?*" insisted Rosher.

A gentle nudge of empathic feeling: *Believe me. Believe me.* And: "If the order had been sent, it would have passed through Chief Communications Officer Norlan. It didn't."

"You have this from Norlan?"

"Yes. Put yourself in his place. What would you do if you knew what he knows?"

A pause. Rosher chewed his lower lip softly. Looked up at her. "How do you know Norlan's not just making all this up?"

With all her mental force, she attempted to open herself up to him. His eyes blinked. He was getting something. "Because of my Talent," she said quietly. "I'm a regular human lie detector. And Norlan didn't lie. I got this information through Leana Coffer, the executive officer."

Briefly, she detailed the situation on the bridge as Coffer had relayed it to her, centering on Darsen's madness and Tamner's virtual control of the *Pegasus*. She buttressed her case by pointing out the common-knowledge facts of Security's dealings with unrest on the ship. As she spoke, the emotions waving at her from him became more positive. She finished up quickly, letting him bring up the reason for their talk.

"Coffer is organizing opposition, isn't she?" said Rosher in a low voice. Co-operative vibrations: he would help.

"What can I do?" Was that a quaver of enthusiasm she felt from him?

"A lot." And she told him exactly what.

Leana Coffer's Journal
(Vocoder transcription authorized
by Leana Coffer. Original recording
voice-locked per program 774-D.)

I've received a report from Mora. Ston Maurtan passed it on to Gary Norlan, who reported to me. She says she has enlisted forty-three crew people—twenty of them officers. Five are assigned to monitoring the ship's computer and doing routine programming—they may be most useful. If they can turn the ship itself against Darsen, we may save lives which would otherwise have been wasted in fighting. Mora also claims eleven command personnel. I'll have to see how many of these I can arrange to have on duty on the bridge and in the chartroom when the rebellion begins. Unfortunately, Mora has recruited only one security officer, a fellow named O'Hari. He should be able to obtain a few hand weapons from the armory, but this will hardly be decisive. Worse, it indicates that most security people are loyal to Darsen—perhaps they're enjoying the new authority that Darsen's paranoia has given them.

It's obvious from Mora's report that we'll need some diversion, to throw Security off balance when we make our move. I have a plan, but it will entail high risks for Mora and Ston. They've been so loyal that I almost can't ask it of them—but if not them, then who?

We must use terrorism.

There's an area of the habitation module particularly vulnerable to sabotage, one which is easily accessible. It's at the bottom of the main lift shaft, just below sleeper deck. If a big enough hole were blown in the hull there, depressurization could occur on every deck accessible to the main lift. This area is also as far from the bridge and engineering sections as any point in the ship.

I want Ston and Mora to position themselves there and threaten the ship. They will claim to have a bomb.

Such a threat will draw off enough Security from the operational sections of the vessel to facilitate our take-over. Ston and Mora are perfect for the role—they're outcasts, with a history of erratic behavior. Further, Security won't dare take direct action against them, for fear of detonating the bomb. If all goes as planned, Ston and Mora won't have to hold out very long. If it doesn't, they're both dead.

But then if my plan fails, we all are.

I've sent them these instructions, using Gary Norlan as a go-between. Now the fate of the *Pegasus* is in their hands.

THIRTEEN

As soon as Mora heard of Coffer's plan from Ston, she took the chance and recontacted one of their six officers in Engineering Maintenance. With very little trouble, she was able to secure a compact metal box, various electronic paraphernalia that Ston had requested, chemicals, a battery, and a laser soldering gun.

While Mora co-ordinated dispersal of the few weapons that Bisc O'Hari had been able to obtain for her, Ston busied himself in her cabin, making his "bomb."

O'Hari was a big, somber, silent man. When Mora had approached him, feeling he was a prime target for enlistment in the mutiny, he had cut short her preliminary conversation and fixed her with his slightly bulging eyes. "You're organizing a mutiny, aren't you?" For a terrifying moment, she thought that perhaps her Talent had played her false, and was certain that the security officer would grab her, toss her before Tamner, and that would be it. "If so," the man continued, "I want in." No explanation. "I think I can get some weapons," he said, after she explained the details. "I'll be sitting in the third row of the Tri-Vid theater this evening. If I am successful, there will be a plastic package underneath the seat when I leave."

Evidently, he had been successful.

In the package she picked up that evening were two laser pistols, and four beam stunners. The lasers were of especial value—generally, not even the security officers were allowed to use the pistols, except for the most extreme emergencies—they carried the beam stunners to render opposition helpless. But the fact that the battery's laser supply had been opened meant that Tamner was getting ready for that extreme emergency, should it arrive.

She kept the lasers for herself and Ston. After all, they would be most vulnerable for the longest period of time. The stunners she stealthily distributed among contactees in Engineering and Com-

puter Control. She assumed that O'Hari could take care of the
bridge.

When she returned from her tense rounds, all four stunners now
in the hands of mutineers, Ston was happily seated at her desk, playing with his new toy.

"It's mostly for effect, actually," he said, pointing out the series of
dummy controls and lights he'd placed on the box. "For the record,
this is a plastimax bomb. Those are easy enough to make, if you've
got the right materials. They'll believe us." He smiled down playfully
at it, chuckling. "The best part of it is that it really *is* a bomb."

"*What?*" cried Mora in disbelief.

"Yeah. Your Engineering Maintenance contact got exactly the
chemicals I wanted for a *smoke* bomb, operative when I press my
remote control button." He held up a little plastic box. "It might
help a lot if we get a bunch of security people breathing down our
necks. Who knows?"

Mora nodded. "Yes. Who knows?" A pang of fear swelled in her.
Fear for herself and Ston. A momentary glimmer on the fringes of
her consciousness: *Smoke. Fighting. Ston.* And then it was gone.

She leaned over and kissed his head. "I love you, Ston."

"Love you too," he said, preoccupied with a bit of wiring.

She sighed. "How will we know when we phase into normal
space? They might not announce it."

"Easy. One of us can sit up on the observation deck. When the
phase begins, so do our operations."

A sudden realization hit her. "Ston! I just realized—we're talking
about everything in the cabin. The bugging monitor—"

"Oh, I forgot to tell you. Don't worry. I found it a couple of days
ago. It's in your intra-ship speaker. Not very original. The first thing
I did when I got these tools was to fix it. Anyone listening now will
just think we're not even in. After we get all this together, I'll switch
it back and . . . and we can act like we just came in, or something.
You think I'd talk about this thing here if I thought Security was listening in?"

"No. I suppose not."

"I don't blame you for being all wound up. You've been doing a
great deal of work, Mora. Now, according to what Norlan told me,
tomorrow's the big day. So why don't you get some sleep, okay? I'll
be finished with this in a little while, and grab some as well. We'll
both be fresh tomorrow."

"Fresh for the slaughter," murmured Mora.

"What was that?" asked Ston absently.

"Nothing." She slipped into bed, was quietly thoughtful for a while. Then, "Ston?"

"Hmmm?"

"If we get back—"

"*When* we get back," he corrected.

"When we get back, to wherever we'll end up, what will happen—with us, I mean?"

He stopped working, turned to look at her. "I told you, we'll stick together, help each other out."

"No, Ston. I mean *us*."

"Oh." He turned back to the box, but did not resume work. "She *is* fading, Mora," he said in a soft voice. "And you're getting stronger inside me. In ways Adria never was. Will that do for now?"

"I guess it will have to," she said.

They had long since reached the center of the Null-R energy vortex, the intertwined Div Harlthor and the ship-being; long since had passed through the manufactured hole in space that had been their destination. Now they waited for those who would greet them, those of *Tin Woodman*'s kind.

Div had learned much. Of the plan, and of its consequences. And, more personally, he had learned more of himself . . . and why he had caused, subconsciously, the *Pegasus* to follow them.

It was all so strange, and yet it explained so much.

They conversed, as they waited.

"Our lives must seem very long to you," said *Tin Woodman*.

"Yes," responded Div. "During the time you orbited Aldebaran, all of human history occurred. So many billions of lives passed, without any understanding . . . of what I've discovered. I never suspected what I was beginning when I grabbed at the chance to escape my prison. Perhaps I did what I did intuitively. I hope more strongly than you can know that I can communicate these things to the humans aboard the *Pegasus*, if they come, if they live . . . the things I've known since I have melded into you."

"You were fulfilling a dream which stretches beyond the beginnings of your race. So am I. Do you know that you have altered my inner world profoundly? I have never had a sense of myself as separate from my symbiote—certainly never with Vul. You are almost insubstantial in so many ways, but you hold to a sense of yourself with great tenacity. By now our merging should be complete. You will not let the existence of *us* consume the knowledge of *you* and *I*. It seems —perverse."

"Does it trouble you?"

"Yes. Very much. And yet I find it stimulating in many ways."

"There is still so much that I do not understand yet. I wonder if I ever will."

"Not as long as you remain 'I.'"

"No doubt your brethren will find me and my kind much different."

"Do not worry, my love. They will accept. They must."

Div considered. "Is there anything that I—*we* can do to assure the safe arrival of the *Pegasus*?"

"We can only sense it at this distance. There is nothing we can do. The internal strife aboard may be fatal . . . the force of the passage may destroy the primitive vessel. No, there is nothing we can do . . . but wait."

Deep inside, Div felt a pang of regret. "We should not have beckoned them . . ."

"You did it out of love. Do not be concerned. We have only to wait."

Time passed. Eventually, the others arrived. There was great joy among them at the return of their long-lost brother. When the link was made, they said, "Come, brother. The journey to our present home is long. We should leave now."

But the creature that was *Tin Woodman* said, "No. We must wait."

The *Pegasus* phased out of its Null-R jump, close to the heart of the galaxy.

Communications Officer Gary Norlan was on the bridge when the starship broke out into normal space.

Normal? he thought. *No. Hardly that, with the stars congested like this* . . .

Soon, if things went right, Coffer's planned diversionary tactic would commence. And on its heels, the mutiny. Coffer was on the bridge herself now, manning the sensor equipment . . . she had wangled that assignment so that she could be on the bridge at this time.

Perched in his padded swivel chair, simultaneously watching the
vu-plates and the crew, Norlan could almost smell the tension. It
was not the odor of perspiration—the air filters would hardly allow
that to last long. It was actually, he realized, not even a smell as
such. Perhaps it was synesthesia working in him—a transmuting of
signals he received on some mental level into a scent.

The captain was standing. Tamner was beside him, arms folded,
calmer in appearance than anyone else.

"All right, Coffer," Darsen said. "You've had enough time. What
do the sensors say?"

"There's a great deal of interference due to the close proximity
with so many suns, Captain," said the woman, not looking up from
her console.

"I didn't ask about interference, Coffer. I want to know if there's
any sign of the alien."

"No, Captain. But there is something rather odd ahead of us." She
looked up. "Readings indicate something like a large black hole. But
there's enough difference to make me doubtful."

Darsen seemed to clutch at this information desperately. Stepping
forward, he leaned over to look at the sensor readings on Genson's
board. "How far away is it?"

"About four hundred thousand kilometers."

Darsen ordered six probe ships to be dispersed to examine the phenomenon closely, telling Engineering to keep the *Pegasus* at the present comparatively slow speed which it had maintained since the end
of its Null-R jump.

Norlan relayed the orders through his communications panel.

They waited.

After a time, Norlan began to worry that everything was not going
well with Ston and Mora. They should have made contact. . . .

The section of his communication banks assigned to connect with
the probes began to flash its lights. Red, blue. Red. Blue.

"We have visual transmission from probes one, four, and six," he
called out. He swiveled his chair to face Darsen, glancing past him
toward Leana Coffer, who appeared quite disturbed.

Now they would find out what Darsen had gotten them into.

"Relay probe one's transmission through to vu-tank controls," Darsen ordered, making fine adjustments on the focus and interference-
masking controls. Finally, a clear picture coalesced in the suspended
holographic globe. The view of space it held was so filled with dis-

tant stars that a pearl-dust glow studded with the brilliance of nearer clusters fairly gleamed in the tank. It was stunningly different from the image of blackness relieved only by random pin points of light which Norlan had always associated with space.

In the very center of the picture was a black spot, fully visible in outline against the general luminescence. Without waiting for an order, the visual control officer increased the magnification on this spot by a factor of ten. The image shimmered and the spot came to dominate it, clearly circular in outline, allowing no light from the stars behind it to shine through.

"It's only about four kilometers in diameter," reported Lieutenant Markos, studying his computer screen, reading the probe telemetry. "And it's absolutely stationary, measured against our galactic navigation grid."

Darsen didn't take his eyes away from the vu-tank. "A neutron star? Or perhaps a black hole . . ." Even at this moment, Norlan could not help judging Darsen, measuring his control over the crew and his resolve. Norlan was pleased at the confusion; speculating aloud as Darsen was doing gave the bridge crew members reason to doubt; something a captain should never allow.

"That's not possible," said Coffer from her sensor console. "Astronomers have mapped most of the gravitational-collapse phenomena in this sector long since, as I'm sure the captain is aware. We've no record of this one. Further, this . . . thing doesn't exert nearly enough attractive force to be either a neutron star *or* a black hole. It does, however, possess enough attraction to continue dragging this ship toward it—which it has just begun doing. Should we take measures?"

Darsen glared at Coffer. "No. Not now. Switch to probe six," he ordered Norlan. "Coffer, you will offer your observations and suggestions when I request them, and only then."

Probe six had been intended to move past the black object but had been pulled into a downward-spiraling orbit around it. When the vu-tank was switched to six's signal it showed essentially the same thing as the first probe: a featureless black disc, motionless in space. As the probe moved around the disc, however, it showed clearly that the thing was actually a sphere.

"Commander Coffer, continue with your report now, please," Darsen said harshly.

"The black sphere absorbs radiation, but does not produce any. Its gravitational influence—assuming that this force is gravity as we understand it—is many times Earth normal. Beyond that, I have no information. Radar and other sensor beams don't return from its surface."

"So it is a hole of some sort after all."

"Yes, Captain, but not belonging to the class of phenomena we call black—" Coffer began.

"Of course not, idiot!" Darsen seemed seized by a wild enthusiasm. "Tamner, what's your evaluation of this thing?"

The lieutenant commander walked around the perimeter of the bridge toward Darsen's desk, looking pleased with himself. "It's probably artificial—but I imagine you've already concluded that yourself. If it is such, though, it's most likely generated by a mechanism of some sort. Since there's no evidence of any such machine in the vicinity, it must be on the other side."

Darsen looked momentarily puzzled. "The other side—the other end of the rift, you mean."

"Precisely."

"We've followed *Tin Woodman*'s trail as closely as possible," Darsen continued excitedly, "and if we hadn't popped out of Null-R just at the edge of the rift's attraction, we'd never have noticed it—it's so small."

"So the rift must have been *Tin Woodman*'s destination—the alien went *through* it!"

Oh, God. He means to follow it, Norlan thought. Desperately, he searched for an argument, any protest which might appeal to Darsen in his fanatical state of mind. Where were Mora and Ston? They had to stall. . . . He looked over at Coffer and read similar thoughts on her face.

His own thoughts were interrupted by the blinking out of probe four's light display.

"Captain, probe four's gone," Genson reported immediately. "It passed straight through the rift."

"You've lost its signal entirely?" Darsen demanded.

"Yes, Captain. It was perfectly clear up until the moment the probe contacted the rift's 'surface.' Then the signal stopped."

"Absorbed by the rift's field," Tamner observed.

"That's one possibility," Norlan said, "one way of looking at it." Tamner stared at Norlan, who stood and looked toward Darsen. "The probe's signals aren't being absorbed," he continued. "Not necessarily. I think the probe has passed out of *range* of our receivers."

"Impossible," said Darsen. "Our equipment has a range of light-years."

It was then that the message from Ston and Mora finally came through.

FOURTEEN

"Priority communication. Repeat—priority." Ston Maurtan released the button and waited for clearance. He smiled and winked at Mora, who stood by the small storage closet where they had placed their "bomb." Mora tried to smile back, but could not. She was concentrating on lending Ston as much emotional support as possible, but it was all she could do to maintain her own in a semblance of steadiness. *Let it be over quickly,* she prayed.

"They're probably wrapped up in searching for *Tin Woodman,*" said Ston. "But I should think that Norlan would be ready for our signal."

Coffer had selected the site well. Immediately below the base of the lift shaft—which made its final stop on the sensor platform, they were in a dimly lit storage room devoted to reserve sensor equipment. There were two points of entry—a set of metal stairs and a large, simple service elevator which moved only back and forth between the storage room and the floor above it. The first thing Ston had done was to cut that elevator's wires. Around and about them were the hulking forms of stacked component boxes on shelves with irregular aisles formed between them.

A *terrorist's paradise,* mused Mora.

"Bridge. Lieutenant Norlan speaking."

Mora could hear Ston swallow, take a deep breath. "I wish to speak to the captain, Mr. Norlan. And the captain only."

"Identify yourself and reason for request."

"My name is Ston Maurtan. I have a bomb."

There was a long moment of silence. *Norlan's playing this very well,* thought Mora.

"Would you repeat that, please."

"I *demand* to speak to Captain Darsen. Immediately."

Another long pause.

Ston licked his lips.

It had all gone well so far. The package they had carried down the lift and into the storage space had not attracted attention from Security. Evidently most of the attention of the crew had been on the imminent breakout into normal space. No one seemed to notice either Mora or Ston, a covered package tucked under his arm. Even the technicians at the controls on the sensor platform were so busy they failed to see the two as they sneaked down the stairway into the room where they stood now. Mora had been assigned the task of awaiting the breakout from Null-R; she had just returned, after being detained by the crush of people moving about the ship to their various stations.

A hard-edged voice issued from the speaker grille. The captain.

"Who is this? Where are you? We've no time for foolish threats. Desist, and we'll forget the whole thing."

Mora saw Ston smile grimly. "And let this gorgeously crafted bomb go to waste? I wouldn't think of it, Captain. I can get so much use out of it."

"I recognize your voice . . ." said Darsen. "Maurtan. Ston Maurtan."

A feeling of *déjà vu* swept through Mora.

"No secret about that, Captain. I identified myself to your man Norlan. But my threats are not frivolous or idle, let me assure you. I've got the hardware and the position to back me up. And the resolve. Also, I might add, a deadman's switch on the bomb's remote control."

"Is Mora Elbrun involved?" Pause. "Just what do you want, Maurtan?"

"This is the situation, Captain," said Ston. "This is what I want."

Coffer watched as the reaction registered on Captain Darsen's face: anger, surprise, fear. From the speaker boxes, Ston Maurtan's voice outlined his position. It was almost better than Coffer had envisioned. But, most important, it was *happening*.

". . . and now that I've told you about the bomb, I'll tell you how you can ensure it doesn't detonate. It will kill me, true—but it will also disable the *Pegasus* in a manner you won't quite be able to deal with, so far away from the Triunion. Quite simply, I want you to turn about and start heading right back the way we came. I think we're all tired of your little game, Darsen. I think we all want to go home and be done with this foolishness you've brought about."

Darsen jammed down on the communicator button. "You're insane, Maurtan!" His eyes, Coffer saw from her station, seemed unsure, but his features held onto their almost single-minded appearance of resolve.

"Perhaps, Captain."

"This must be a bluff," said Darsen breathlessly. His eyes sought out Tamner's. Tamner nodded, unemotionally. A scowl of disbelief lined his face.

"No, Captain," continued the radio voice. "Not a bluff. I've got nothing to lose—and much to gain. After all, you had no business ordering this ship after the alien, did you now? You know as well as I do you received no such orders from Galactic Command. In fact, you can almost say I'm acting on their behalf."

"You have no right to carry on this way in *my* ship!"

"Oh—it's your ship, is it? Not the Triunion's? Is that what you're saying?" the voice teased. "Well, no matter. It's all one. Now as it happens, I also have weapons down here. And sufficient food and water to last for some time. Plus a companion to relieve me if I want to sleep. All I ask is that you simply go back to where we began. Back to where we belong. I won't be unreasonable. You have thirty minutes to consult with your command officers. Perhaps you can even take a vote among the crew. But I warn you, if I don't get the answer I want, I'll press this little button right away. Understood?"

Darsen leaned forward tiredly. "Yes. Yes. Understood." He motioned to Norlan to cut off the channel, then turned to face Tamner. The entire bridge crew was silent, all eyes resting on Darsen. In the screens the dazzles of the myriad stars seemed to grow more intense —as though they were a million other eyes, straining to peer into the scene of this peculiar drama.

"Absolutely impossible, Captain," declared Tamner, striding up to Darsen. "There's no way they could have made any kind of bomb. The necessary elements are not available."

Captain Darsen clenched his fists in frustration. "There was no way for Maurtan to get off this ship with Mora Elbrun, either. But he *did* it. I just don't know . . ." His heels squeaked as he turned to Coffer at her sensor console. "What do *you* say, Coffer? If a bomb tears apart that portion of the hull, will the lower half of the ship depressurize?"

She was surprised that he sought her advice after virtually ignoring her for so long. "Hard to say, Captain. We don't know what sort of impact the bomb would have—if indeed it's a bomb." She could not take any hard stand, she realized. This might be some sort of test. "It seems to me that if it *is* a bomb, and the man does set it off, the principal problem will be that it's certain to wipe out all the main sensor banks—not to mention the occupants of sleeper deck. And if the device is what Maurtan claims it is—well, there's no way we can seal off the levels immediately, or for that matter, well enough."

"Look, Captain," exclaimed Tamner, now furious. "They've given us time to deal with them, even if there *is* a bomb. Let me take a detachment of Security down right away. We'll take care of them in short order. Meanwhile, take your precautions—"

"You're right, damn it!" Darsen's face grew red with his passion. "If we don't take care of this *now*, nip it in the bud, we'll have problems like this throughout the ship. We can't take that chance. We've come one hell of a distance—and we're *not* going to abandon our goal just because of a ridiculous threat." He turned to Tamner. "Do what you must, Commander. I've entrusted inner ship security to you. You may handle this matter in any damned way you like."

"Right." Tamner jumped up toward Norlan, brusquely elbowed him aside, and punched out security code. The man ordered up a detachment of twenty-five security officers, instructing the battery guards to break out a suitable complement of weapons. Lasers. Coffer felt a chill of fear for Ston and Mora.

The meeting place of the security men would be sensor deck.

Darsen focused his attention back upon the enigma before them, ordering a wary but steady approach toward the rift.

Not much time, thought Coffer. *I'll give Tamner ten minutes to get out of the way before I act.*

At Darsen's orders, she directed her attention back to the sensor readouts. But peripherally she watched as Tamner stormed out of the bridge, murderous intent quite visible on his features.

That left two security officers on the bridge.

And one of them was Bisc O'Hari.

"Put your pistol on 'full,'" said Ston, adjusting his own as he leaned against a wall after making the final check of his mechanism in the closet. "Much as I hate the idea of killing anyone, we're not playing games here. They certainly intend to kill *us*. We'll extend the same consideration."

Mora nodded grimly. She looked down at her weapon. It was a

compact ovoid fitted with a trigger handle and a small black nozzle from which the coherent light would emanate. She had never fired one before, let alone *shot* anyone, she thought.

"They'll be charging down that metal staircase," Ston was saying, stalking about excitedly like some animal before it begins the hunting of its prey. "We've got the advantage on them there. Have you got your mask? They might try to throw some sort of gas in—or maybe feed it through the ventilation system. No telling *what* they'll do—but whatever it is, they'll try to accomplish it as fast as possible. And when they find out our bomb threats have been empty— well, we're *really* going to have to fight for our lives." He made a quick scan of the area. "We'd best position ourselves." After directing Mora to stand behind a metal abutment which afforded a thick screen from laser fire, he situated himself beneath a shelf, the base of which lent him similar protection. In his right hand he held his weapon, safety off; in his left was the remote control device which would detonate the smoke bomb, his finger on the deadman switch.

They waited.

Her chronometer showed that five minutes had passed since Ston had finished delivering his ultimatum. To Mora, it seemed much longer than that. Doubts raged in her mind. Chances were, they might be killed. And would this diversion really matter in the long run? Was it worth it? Perhaps Ston should have refused Coffer's request. Maybe they should have played it safe, kept their heads low throughout the whole affair.

But she knew that Ston would have had none of *that*. And, she admitted to herself, they had done what they had to.

There was a sudden squeak from down the aisle. A ragged hum of malfunctioning machinery.

"They're trying the service elevator," said Ston. "Good thing the operation wires are down here, or they could fix them. This way they have to come down a couple at a time—and very carefully."

Those noises ceased.

She and Ston were on opposite sides of the aisle which ended at the base of the stairway from the sensor platform. Mora had a clear view of its doorway. She drew a bead on it, practicing.

The moments passed. The silence grew thick, oppressive.

When the sound finally came, it was like a shattering explosion, even though it was only the door at the top of the stairs being opened.

Mora braced herself.

The steady, metallic clop clop clop of feet hitting stairsteps descended on them, like a droning, toneless bell of doom.

But it was only one set of feet. Only one person was coming down. No furious rush of scrabbling boots, no clicking of weapons. Only the steady clop clop clop.

Suddenly, Mora was aware of the heavy scent of her own perspiration. It smelled like fear.

A dark shadow bulked suddenly large in the doorway. It took a step closer, and the dark shadow's face seemed to resolve from vague darkness into recognizable human features.

The features of Lieutenant Commander Jin Tamner.

He wore no body armor. His arms were raised, his hands empty. About his waist was a holster. His laser pistol was in that holster. There was no expression on his face.

"I've come to talk with you," he said, simply. Mora could see his eyes glancing about, trying to pin-point their locations. "You *are* here, aren't you?"

Ston spoke. "Oh yes. We're here. We asked that no one should come down here. You're lucky we haven't killed you. You're even luckier that we haven't interpreted this as a hostile action, and triggered the bomb."

"Hostile?" Tamner waved a hand slightly. "I present no threat to you at the moment. I'm out in the open. You're well protected. I'm not even quite sure where you are. The lighting isn't all that great down here. No. No threat. The captain sent me down to reason with you. You chose a very inopportune time for this little, foolish game. The *Pegasus* is on the verge of perhaps the greatest accomplishment in human history. We'll all be renowned for this exploit. Why should we mar it with this little business?"

"Is that what you're after, Tamner?" said Ston. "Fame? A feeling of importance? Is *this* why you've aided Darsen's stupid, foolish quest so loyally?"

The man shrugged. "I'd hardly qualify *that* as the only reason, but I wouldn't dismiss it as part of it. But that's neither here nor there in our discussion. I've come here to parlay with you. Come to terms. Most likely, you haven't *got* a bomb stashed away down here. The whole idea is stupid, childish. We hardly think you'd sacrifice your lives and kill hundreds, just to alter this ship's course. You and Mora —yes, she *is* down here, isn't she?—aren't the wisest individuals I've ever encountered. But neither are you the maniacs you'd like us to believe you are now. No. I interpret this as just another of your bids for attention. And so does the captain. We're willing to forgive. So why don't you just come along with me, peacefully. We'll have to lock you in the brig for a time. But just long enough to see that you don't interfere with this delicate situation we on the bridge find ourselves in. And then we'll let you go, and attribute this rash, foolish threat to the strain we've all been under. We won't record it—no one else will ever know. All you have to do is to come out, and come with me. That's all we ask—and in reward for your co-operation, Galactic Command will never find out."

"Galactic Command will be lucky to know *anything*," returned Ston bitterly. "I'd rather be in their hands, safe in our home sector of space, than rushing toward infinity and uncertainty out here. I'll let *them* be the judge of our actions. Not you, not Darsen."

"Just talking with you, I know you're not mad, Maurtan. You don't sound like someone who would trigger a device that would destroy hundreds of human lives, and endanger hundreds more." He turned his head slightly, nodded. Smoothly, two security officers stepped out of the doorway, drew up to his side. Both wore laser holsters. Both also had their hands raised in a manner similar to Tamner's. Mora had not heard them descend, had not even sensed their presence until now. And they were too far away to take an empathic reading on their intent.

"Just consider these two part of my diplomatic envoy, Maurtan," continued Tamner, attempting his version of a friendly smile. "No need for alarm whatsoever."

"Why don't you just bring down *all* your men, Tamner," replied Ston. "A thousand officers couldn't stop me from releasing this switch if I decide to. According to my reckoning, the captain has over ten minutes to respond, personally, to my demands. I intend to let him have the benefit of every single minute."

Tamner frowned. "We don't intend to play games with you, Maurtan. I assure you that the captain has entrusted me entirely with this matter. I think it would be of benefit to both of us to discuss the situation like reasonable human beings."

"Very well," Ston replied. "But I suggest that you not make any unnecessary movements toward your weapons. We *are* armed."

"Ah yes. You and Mora. Where did you get the weapons, I wonder? Did you turn yourself invisible, sneak past the battery guards? I doubt it—I doubt if you've weapons of significance at all. And, Mora —why are you doing this? Trying to get back at us? Surely you realize that we've gone too far to turn back now. We're committed. However you feel about us, whatever you think we've done to you, surely you can't take it out on the whole ship. Because that's what you're—"

He was interrupted by the sudden blaring of the room's general address speaker.

Mora instantly recognized the voice.

It was Norlan's.

"All ship's personnel, alert."

Even as he spoke into the microphone that curled around on its metal stalk, rearing like a spitting cobra before him, Norlan glanced down at his control panel for another check. It was vital that his voice reach every section of the ship, issue from every available speaker. Fifteen minutes had passed since Tamner had rushed off the bridge. In that time, Captain Darsen had turned all of his attention back to preparing the ship for entrance through the spatial anomaly before them—the rift. And Coffer had given the signal . . .

Good. All the appropriate switches were on.

"All crew members, take emergency measures. Passengers, secure yourselves in turbulence harnesses and gravity couches."

And the strange black spot in the view screens before them, the sphere of pure darkness that contrasted so with the generous scatter of stars in this sector, grew as they neared it. Norlan knew that if they got too close, the *Pegasus* would be hard-pressed to outpower the thing's tremendous gravitational pull and escape from being drawn through it into the unknown. Who knew what would happen then? Perhaps they would be torn apart by the tremendous forces this strange hole in space seemed to own. And if they *did* survive the passage—where would they be? And would they be able to return?

He had been so desperate, he was about to take action before he had any specific orders from the captain for the ship-wide address he had expected, informing the crew of their present circumstances. From his occasional glances to Coffer, he could see that she was growing nervous as well. Her eyes, when they connected with his, seemed to say, "When? When?"

But finally, upon his suggestion, Captain Darsen had allowed that it would be necessary to take safety precautions, should the entrance through the rift be turbulent. He ordered him to notify the rest of the crew and passengers.

"Possible gravitational fluctuations and confusion. Repeat, please take emergency measures."

He took a breath and prayed that it was not too late.

And that the plan would work.

"Compliments of the captain."

". . . of the captain."

The final words dropped like a mild pronouncement of doom from the speaker perched almost directly over the top of his station. His head jerked up from the flashing readings on his fusion ramjet monitor. He had been expecting those words, indeed ardently praying for their arrival. His job in Engineering supplied him with full knowledge of the position and destination of the *Pegasus*. If the mutiny were held off much longer, it well might be useless.

Nevertheless, when the words finally came on the tail of the announcement of the emergency, they startled Ensign Dinni Rosher. The weight of guilt settled fully on his shoulders as he realized the totality of the implications of his intended actions. His years of training at the academy suddenly drew rein on his rebel mind, and brought him up short. No, he *couldn't*. A violent overthrow of the authority that governed his life, on such flimsy notice? How did he know that he wasn't the only one that strange woman had contacted? How did he know that he wouldn't be immediately overpowered, the sole mutineer? Overpowered, stashed away to rot until court-martial—maybe even *killed* in the scuffle!

Quivering slightly, he let his eyes roam over his fellows seated at their positions in the room, over the pair of security men by the doors. And he saw his own fear and trepidation mirrored in the eyes of Lieutenant Markle. In the expression of Ensign Mitters. And in at least two others of the ten officers stationed there. They seemed as hesitant as he—it was almost as if they were experiencing the same emotions. Undergoing the same doubts.

As he leaned back in his chair, astonished, he felt the hard plastic and metal of the stunner taped to the small of his back press against his spine: a sharp jolt of pain reminded him of his role. It was as though that knife of sensation punctured the dam of doubt. His former feelings, his resolve, flooded back in full measure. And once again the Talent, Mora, seemed to touch his mind. *It's the right thing to do*, she seemed to say. *And it must be done immediately.*

He pulled the seal release on the side of his jumpsuit, reached in, tore the stunner off his back. It hurt. But the sting cleared his senses even more. Yes, it must be done now, and with no hesitation, or it would all be lost.

Gripping the pistol, he rose up from the chair, took two steps forward. He leveled the stunner at the closest security officer, a stout, sleepy-eyed man, and fired. The weapon throbbed; energy coursed out, enveloped the man, who shuddered and dropped. His fellow officer was obviously equipped with years of training, for his weapon was instantly being grappled from his holster. But too late. Rosher swung the stunner, fired, and the other security officer crumpled to the floor with a grunt of disbelief.

Rosher strode to the door mechanism, punched in the proper lock sequence as Mora had instructed him. He picked up the unconscious officers' weapons, then looked around at the others.

Several merely stared at him, surprise and horror clear in their aspects. These he would have to watch.

"Stop the engines!" he ordered, waving his stunner. "And be prepared to engage them again on my orders."

But the four he had noticed before had already commenced that operation.

"Compliments of the captain."

So.

Then Mora Elbrun had told the truth. A flicker of good feeling trembled at the edges of Secondary Programmer Avedon Avedic's mind. She had liked the former shiplady, indeed felt an affinity with the woman. It was interesting. Mora seemed to be successful in doing something that the service had never been able actually to do: get its members together on something, of their own free will. Of course, the running of the starships would be impossible if the crew members did not co-operate. But co-operation under the tyranny of rules and orders was an entirely different affair from the sort of co-operation that Mora seemed to be linking together. This was a distinct action *against* orders, rules, and laws. In the eventual interest of the service, true—if indeed this matter of Captain Darsen's insanity was the case; if he had spirited the *Pegasus* on this wild, breakneck course to the center of the galaxy. The thought appealed to the dark, comely woman. In fact it pleased her all to hell.

To strike back at Them—with their own instruments, the devices they had trained her to operate. . . .

There wasn't the slightest hesitation on her part. Joyfully, she leaned over the keyboard, her long black hair wisping down along the sides of her Mediterranean features. She punched in the codes she had devised—the key that would allow her entrance into the computer's navigational systems. It had taken her a long time to figure out how to do that—longer certainly than the notice from Mora Elbrun had given her. But fortunately she had puzzled out the complex systems of the ship's computer months before. There wasn't much else of comparable interest for a computer freak on this ship.

Feverishly, she typed. And, as she always knew they would, the ghostly, ephemeral figures that swept over the read-out screen were responding with the proper sequences.

She had never really wanted to enlist in the service at first. All she had wanted was to get her hands on computer circuitry—it was her life. With computers, there were endless possibilities—riddles to unravel, puzzles to doodle over endless rapturous hours—and in the end new and better machines. Back on Earth, her enthusiasm had been boundless. She had zipped through her technical and theoretical training, had met all the myriad requirements for any of the topflight research institutes. Indeed her qualifications had been so great that she expected to be able easily to vault over the little setbacks of her political affiliations. So what if she'd lent her voice to the collective outcry against her government? Surely that would not hurt her. It was supposed to be a free nation.

But all of the computer corporations had turned her down with apologetic mumbles, suggesting that she might try her luck on a colony. But she had no desire to journey to some backwater world—for one thing, their machines were just too primitive. It would be like playing with blocks.

And then the service had come to her. How would you like to work on a truly sophisticated and eminently practical computer system? they had cooed, building up the benefits of service life. See the stars. Be important.

She had said no, at first. But her love for computers was great. Immersing herself in math and electronics and all the corollary aspects of computer science that were predictable and yet exciting was so much better than her wretched personal relationships. Computers she could handle. She could love them, and they her—in their own way. It wasn't so with people.

But she had not been getting much of a chance to work on applied computer science theory here. She had to make do with this limited and closed-minded little nothing of a functional starship computer. And so she had learned every centimeter of its components by volunteering for maintenance work from time to time. It was now her baby.

Now it awoke to her touch.

NAVIGATIONAL GRID—∅11∅ IN OPERATION.

Superb.

Suddenly, she was aware of the sounds of violence about her in the low-ceilinged, light-sprinkled room. She had to work fast.

MAINTAIN STAND-BY FOR SPECIFIC ORDERS she tapped into the keyboard.

Making sure her earphone was working properly, clear for orders from the mutiny's contingent on the bridge, she breathed deeply.

A man staggered out from behind a block of machinery. A security officer. He groped for a hold on the block's console. His hand slipped. He tumbled to the floor, his eyes filming over.

Following him, a stunner clutched in hand, came Primary Programmer Lieutenant Birt Mikal. His stark, serious brown eyes found hers.

She smiled at him and laughed, indicating her computer screen. "I just need orders from downstairs."

He smiled back. "Good. Conspiracies are no fun on your own, are they?"

FIFTEEN

"Compliments of the captain."

Hidden behind the shadowy abutment, Mora could not contain a small sigh of relief as Norlan's final phrase receded to a dim echo in the rear of the storage room. The trigger phrase had been issued. The mutiny had begun.

She shot Ston a look, pulsed him a wave of emotion that said, *It is done.*

But the expression on Ston's face returned the truth: No, it wasn't finished at all. It had only begun.

Mora craned her neck back a bit to get a better look at the three security officers. A frown etched deep in his features, the middle man, Tamner, seemed very uneasy. Not at all the former cool, diplomatic emissary he had arrived as.

"You see," he said, shifting from foot to foot, peering into the dimness. "Your threat is too late, anyway. Whether you know it or not, we're headed into a rift of space—following the alien. There's nothing you can do now." He mouthed the words with a finality that lacked conviction. Eying his subordinates hesitantly, he whispered something. He shook his head, worried, and grabbed up his belt communicator. "Security channel. Security channel," he spoke into the disc. "Is everything all right? Do you read me?"

Instantly Mora knew—*felt*—that Tamner suspected. If he managed to reach a member of Security who was witnessing a segment of the mutiny then he would immediately order his detachment up the lift. Something had to be done. The man obviously had no real worry now about the bomb threat—perhaps he never had. He had come down here personally to kill them, be rid of her and Ston once and for all, armed with valid provocation. But now Mora could tell from his eyes and in the vague waves of feeling emanating from him that Jin Tamner was coming to the realization that he'd been had.

Something had to be done to stop him, or at least detain him.

She raised her weapon, reluctantly but without pause for consideration. She fired. A stream of energy singed through the air, struck the communicator full on. There was a flash of explosion. Tamner was hurled back against a bulkhead like a rag doll. His associates toppled aside, sprawling onto the metal floor.

She turned to Ston. He gave her one second of steady, meaningful gaze, then brought up his remote control device.

And released the switch.

"Compliments of the captain."

Gary Norlan pressed off the intercom switches. He directed his gaze to Coffer, still behind her control board, tensely ready. Coffer peered up directly to where Bisc O'Hari stood sentry by the other security officer.

She nodded at him.

The others of the bridge crew were too busy to notice what was happening. Except the captain.

"Mr. Norlan," he said, stepping down from his command desk dais, still keeping part of his attention on the awesome sights before them in the flat screens and the vu-tank. "That was quite good. But you didn't need to mention me." Then as Darsen focused his full attention on Norlan, the captain's face revealed a sudden foreboding premonition. Norlan, expressionless, met his eyes defiantly.

Perplexity plain on his face, Darsen scanned the bridge. Only four of the operational officers were carrying on as before. The others were speedily punching new orders into their control boards. "What's going on here?" he growled. Darsen spun on his heel to summon Security. Immediately there was a harsh buzzing sound, then a crackling whisper. One of the security officers slumped to the deck. His own weapon had not been drawn.

Bisc O'Hari, holding up his stunner, turned to face the captain. "I suggest you follow Commander Coffer's orders now, Darsen." He let his stern gaze include the entire bridge crew. "I suggest that *all* of you do as Norlan says." His upheld weapon waved a bit, underlining the authority of his words.

Mouth open in frank disbelief, Captain Darsen stood still.

"Cease propulsion toward rift," said Coffer immediately. "Be prepared for a complete turnabout, on my orders." She jumped up and moved over toward Norlan's communication board to contact the computer room, the engine room, and the other centers of the mutiny for supporting action. O'Hari, she noticed peripherally, was already busy jamming access to the lift entrance. Good. The bridge was all hers now. Surprisingly swiftly at that. If Tamner had been there—

A hand clutched her arm before she could make it behind the communications console. The captain, face in a rictus of hate and fury, trembled before her. He raised a fist to smash into her but the blow was thwarted by Norlan, who grabbed Darsen's arm. Darsen hurled him away and jumped up to the communications board, attempting to scream his commands into the microphone: "This is Captain Darsen. There is a mutiny occurring on the bridge. There—"

Quickly, O'Hari swung about and blasted. Darsen fell, bending the microphone stalk, more like some ugly discarded manikin than the captain of a huge starship. He pounded onto the floor, unconscious.

"Thanks," said Coffer, trying to rub the pain out of her arm as she moved to the communications console.

The rebel security officer, striding over to be sure of Darsen's harmlessness, grunted. He looked down at the captain with contempt. Vaguely, Coffer wondered what went on in the man's mind; what had goaded him into throwing off years of training to toss his lot in with a bunch of mutineers. She dismissed the thought, merely thankful for the man's invaluable aid. She turned her attention to the rest of the crew. "All right. I'm sure most of you Mora Elbrun contacted and enlisted in our cause. But in any case, all of you must comply. Any deviation from this will be dealt with swiftly by Mr. O'Hari."

The look of blank surprise in some of the faces melted into agreement. Their eyes seemed to flash relief even as they attended to obeying Coffer's orders. The others had long since begun.

Satisfied, Coffer turned back to the controls and proceeded to contact Engineering.

The bomb exploded.

It was not a loud explosion, nor was it violent. It was not intended to be. It was meant only to cause confusion. Ston had left the closet door sufficiently ajar so that at the impact of the bomb it would burst open. It did. Voluminous clouds of black and gray poured freely from the closet and, like a sudden fog, began to stream their opacity over everything.

Before the smoke covered them, Mora saw the security officers struggling to their feet, brandishing their weapons. Before long the crowd of the other security officers would flow down the stairs, into the fray. All to the good. She could see Ston's intention; while a good portion of Security was busy searching for them down here, the mutiny could continue apace above.

A flash of light streaked illumination through the cloudbound base of the stairway: a laser gun.

"Okay, Mora," Ston called in a low voice. "Split up. Keep them guessing. The smoke should drift this way. Use the mask I gave you." He immediately turned, ran down the aisle.

Mora looked up and decided on her course. Slipping her gun into a pocket, she gripped the siding of the shelves and began to pull herself up among the stored equipment. The top attained, some five meters above the floor, she positioned herself, pulled out her gun, and looked down. The smoke was billowing out swiftly, mushrooming up. She could smell it. She put on the filter mask Ston had given her should this eventuality occur. The sounds of the security officers emerging from the doorway, coughing, came to her. She debated firing down into their midst, decided against it. She had no real desire to harm anyone, and her laser track would be sure to pin-point her location. No. Best to hide, to fire only in defense. It was better to stall that confrontation as long as possible, thus lengthening the time the officers were oblivious to the situation topside.

Already the smoke was spreading, thinning itself out throughout the room, becoming more translucent. It simmered up to her, covering her legs. It was being drawn through the air ducts.

She made sure her filter mask was properly adjusted over her mouth and nose, crouched down low, watching carefully. The clamor and confusion from below drifted up in greater volume as more security men descended. As the smoke lessened, she could see their vague figures searching the aisles like vengeful ghosts. There were enough of them now, and they were close enough, that she began to feel their emotional presences: hate, laced with fear and a sense of duty. She tried to block it all out, but was not entirely successful.

Their emotions quickly smothered the small empathic contact she had with Ston. This triggered a response, and suddenly she remembered.

The dream.

The dream she had dreamed over and over, in the Henderson. The strange battle. It flooded back into her memory, every gloomy detail of it, dragging its ominous sensations with it as starkly and vividly as she'd experienced them in slumber. But her somnambulent vision carried new meaning. Now, it made sense.

The moment she recalled her fear for Ston, it was as though someone had punched her in the stomach. Her fear for him drove all else from her mind. A feeling of terrible dread enveloped her. She forgot any regard for her own safety.

Standing up, she tried to reach out with her Talent and touch him. To warn . . . *Be careful,* she pulsed, translating the literal meaning into their underlying emotional meaning. But she felt no response, no touch of his answer.

Hastily, she picked her way down to the opposite end of the shelving top, over a scatter of boxes. With little regard for the possibility of a fall, she let herself down the edge, stepped onto the next level. Recklessly, she lowered herself down the next two levels into the thicker haze and jumped the rest of the way, landing off balance, thumping to the floor. The gun in her pocket popped out, skittered away. She scrambled over, lifted it up. Rising, she peered into the smoke searching for Ston.

There remained the tumultuous clamor of pounding feet all around. Dimly, she could see shapes running in the near distance.

Suddenly, far down the other side of the room, the smoke became veined with lines of energy. The light lances flickered like straightened bolts of lightning. Screams, yells cried out from the same direction.

They had found Ston.

Instantly, she raced down the aisle toward them.

And then the beams of light ceased. The noise quieted.

And the pain hit her.

She woke to a terrible sense of loss, of grief, of something beyond the scope of her understanding. And she woke to rough, unsympathetic hands jostling her up from where she had fallen, paralyzed, as Ston had died.

Looking up she saw the security men who were dragging her across the floor. Her first reaction was to struggle. But, reaching for the necessary energy, she found herself drained of resources. Her empathic death had left her listless.

Ston, she thought. *Ston.*

Abruptly, the men stopped. She looked about and saw that the other security officers crowded around as well. Craning her neck with difficulty, she realized that they stood by the slumped form of Jin Tamner. Hovering over Tamner were two men, administering first aid.

"Is he conscious?" a security guard asked.

"Just barely," muttered one of the men attending to their fallen commander. "His hands are shreds. The explosion shrapneled hell out of his torso. I've sent a message for MedSec emergency, but something strange seems to be happening up there."

Tamner spasmed. Mora could see the streams of glistening red, the streaks of charred uniform and flesh from the flash of Mora's laser. Looking down, she was surprised that she felt no more hate for Jin Tamner, nor satisfaction with what she had done. She felt no emotion at all.

Tamner's half-closed bedimmed eyes brightened a bit; intelligence looked up through bars of pain. Those bloodshot orbs swung round, surveying the men and woman who looked down at him. He tried to speak. The officers giving first aid admonished him to stop. Instead, Tamner tried harder, and began creating almost coherent sentences.

". . . damn it . . . get up to the bridge . . . there's something going on . . . don't . . . don't stay down here." He tried to sit up. "That's why they shot the communicator . . . didn't want us to find out. This . . . this must have been a distracting tactic." He gulped in a swallow of air. "Mutiny, God damn it. Maybe a mutiny." Exhausted, he fell back limply into the arms of his attendants. The others looked at one another, bemused. "We'd better check," said one, and all except for the two guarding Mora rushed up the stairway.

No matter, thought Mora. *Too late now, anyway.*

As if she cared.

She looked down at Tamner and realized that he was close to death. Slightly, she opened to him. His eyes fluttered open, fixed on her fuzzily. He smelled of charred flesh. The eyes registered pure and simple hate—but not necessarily focused directly on Mora. No, she realized with a detached curiosity, looking down on the man with her eyes and her Talent as well. No—it was a generalized, unspecific hate. Puzzled, she reached down deeper.

She had never before considered Jin Tamner a subject—merely an object of her hate. His surface attitude was always contemptible. He had brought her only the worst sort of mental anguish in her dealings with him. She had always associated him with the extremes of pain brought on her by the hate of the Normals.

But nothing mattered now. She pushed past that veil of hate in Tamner's mind, delved deeper than she'd ever been before as she stood there with the security men holding her upright, waiting for orders on what to do with her.

Tamner's eyes opened wide. "No," he said, "don't."

Vocally she soothed, "You're dying. I only wish to comfort."

"Let me die alone, then," he said. "Take—" Weak and confused, he couldn't finish the command.

The men holding her started to pull her toward the stairs. "No," she said. "Please—I won't do anything."

Suddenly the intercom announced: "Security alert. Security alert! All—" and was cut off.

"Get out of here," said Tamner. "Both of you." He had roused again. "I *told* you it was a mutiny. They'll need every man. I'll be okay."

"But, sir . . ."

"God damn it, I said I'll be okay."

"But the woman . . ."

"Leave her. She can't do any harm. Just get *out. Now.*"

They obeyed, leaving Mora free and alone with Tamner. But her mind remained active, and once again it probed Tamner's. He seemed too weak to object.

"Why do you hate me?" she asked mildly. She glided into his mind softly, into a dark and twisted place.

He gave no response. She drifted down further into his feelings, his soul, looking for the answer there. That answer never mattered before. The effect of that awful hate was more than enough to be preoccupied with. But now that effect was no longer a consideration —the cause came to the forefront of her interest. Nor was it just the cause of Tamner's hate—she felt a need to know the reason for the irrational fear of other Normals. Perhaps a clue might be discovered in this man, might be more evident, since his hate for Talents was especially strong.

She felt the waves of hatred buffet her as she descended deeper— deeper than she had ever gone into such an inhospitable mind. She had gone beyond the threshold of pain—now she could shrug it off as though it were nothing. At least for a time. Perhaps, she thought, it's a mental numbness . . .

Through the stew of his mind, she swam. And even as she did, she tried to comfort. Her hatred of Tamner had disappeared with the rest of her emotions. Now all that was left was her curiosity.

When she finally withdrew, she was shaking.

"Satisfied?" said Tamner in a barely audible voice. "You've finally gotten into my mind."

She did not respond.

"Trying to sully a man's soul—his pride. His *individuality*," continued Tamner. "You want our souls." His head lolled. His breathing became more shallow. "I am the captain of *this* ship," he whispered. "I—and no one else."

"I—I think I understand now," said Mora. "But you're *wrong*. You're *all* wrong."

Her words fell on deaf ears. The man was dead.

Mora was not sure of it until she crawled over and felt his pulse; she had felt nothing of his dying.

The doors of hell are locked from the inside.

Where had she read that? Now it made a terrible tragic sense to her. This was the way all Normals were, in one degree or another. Tight, constricted, scared—living in their own little dungeons, making only occasional forays out into reality for scraps of communication and love from their fellows.

This was why they hated Talents—those freaks who had skeleton keys to everyone's doors. Who threatened to draw mankind out of their safe, comfortable, private darknesses. Who were frightening in their implications.

And the thing most frightening to all of them was the idea that *they* might also bear the seeds of Talent—that within them there was a kernel of potentiality that would change them from the familiar into the unknown.

Hence, they could not acknowledge that Talents were as human as they were.

She had seen all this in Tamner. And she had felt pity and compassion for him. But it was the curse of his sort that such things as pity and compassion were signs of weakness, and to be disdained.

And thus, he had died alone. As he had lived alone.

There was more to ponder, but Mora was weary. She felt like a castaway, drifting on the open sea, alone after a shipwreck. She found an island of rest and pulled herself up on its shore.

Coffer, eschewing the command desk, maintained her position behind the communications console, waiting for the verdict from Engineering.

The mutiny had not been without casualties on both sides. That much had filtered down to the bridge from the various sites of the *coup*. And, although its success seemed certain, with the mutineers now in control of the necessary function areas of the *Pegasus*, it was by no means over. Coffer had just delivered a ship-wide address, speaking briefly of the situation that had caused the disruption in leadership and the necessity for it. She had no idea whether or not the entire crew had accepted the situation. For all she knew, the remainder of Security might yet be seeking entrance to the bridge.

But all this was comparatively unimportant at the moment. Right now priority consideration had to be given to the situation of the *Pegasus* relative to the space rift. For while the mutiny had progressed, so had the starship—closer and closer to the aperture in space Darsen had directed it toward.

And now the *Pegasus* was in the grip of its tremendous gravitational pull.

The communicator bleeped. Engineering.

"Yes," said Coffer.

"In response to your question about the Null-R jump, Captain. There's no way we can slide into it with this kind of gravitational pull working on us. We have to get out of that first."

"I'd hoped that the gravity would be insufficient."

"Never encountered anything like it. Playing haywire with the instruments. I'm sure ship's computer will tell you the same thing," said the engineering officer. "We managed to position the ship for the ion-drive—"

"Well, damn it," cried Coffer. "Get us out of here. It's only a matter of minutes before that hole swallows us up. Start the engines."

"That's just it," replied the voice contritely. "They've been on for the last minute. We've slowed the descent into the gravity well. But not by much."

Coffer swiveled her attention to Norlan. "Is that true?"

Norlan nodded, looking down at instruments.

Coffer leaned back over to the microphone. "Full acceleration, then."

"We've got the engines working as hard as they can, Captain."

Helplessly, Coffer pounded the console before her. She looked up at a vu-plate. The black of the rift now dominated the screen, like ink slowly spreading out over a pool of stars.

There was nothing more that could be done.

Even though he had lost the battle of the mutiny, Captain Darsen may well have won the war.

The giant maw of the space rift neared.

PART FOUR:

DISCOVERIES

"I have touched the highest point of all my greatness;
 And, from that full meridian of my glory,
 I haste now to my setting: I shall fall
 Like a bright exhalation in the evening,
 And no man see me more."

—William Shakespeare
HENRY VIII, ACT III

SIXTEEN

Every fitting and seam of the *Pegasus* seemed to squeal with stress as the ship plunged into the lightless emptiness of the rift. "We're being crushed!" cried Norlan, voicing Coffer's own fear. She felt as though hundreds of gravities pressed in on her. Yet although she could barely move, the pressure was causing no obvious injury.

A flash of light bright as the heart of a sun blinded her. She heard the ship's overloaded external sensors click off—

The sensation of acceleration disappeared. The lights on the sensor board flashed back on. How long would this passage take—and how far? The vu-tank revealed only blackness—no, there was a star, bright and distant. As her vision cleared, Coffer could pick out a second, then a third star. The ship was in normal space again, then the rift had propelled them almost instantly to this place—wherever this was.

Hesitantly, Coffer sat back down at the communications console. The intercom board was jammed with incoming calls. She switched to the emergency override. "This is Acting Captain Leana Coffer. Attention all crew. Please remain calm. There is no cause for alarm."

The hell there isn't, she thought. But it sounded good.

"We have just passed through a spatial discontinuity we've tagged a 'space rift' for lack of a better term. The passage caused no apparent breech of our vacuum-tight integrity—" She paused, glancing for reassurance at the console warning lights. "I repeat, there is no present cause for alarm. Please commence with your reports."

They began. Evidently, the mutiny had gone surprisingly well, all in all.

After a time, Norlan said, "If you can tear yourself away from the victory reports, Leana, we have a problem with navigation." Coffer looked up to see the man standing over her. "We can't get a course reading. Just look at the vu-tank!"

The sphere had finally resolved into a clear picture. The contrast to the previous points the *Pegasus* had occupied on the other side of the rift was remarkable. Obviously they were on the edge of some galaxy.

But *what* galaxy?

And so very few stars. Somewhat larger than the stars were a number of hazy, glowing discs, grouped together in the middle of the tank. Galaxies? *Clusters* of galaxies?

"Oh, God," said Coffer. "Where are we?"

"*That* is what the navigation board can't tell us," replied Norland.

"Perhaps it needs more data. Have Lieutenant Volfe start feeding new data to the chart computers." She commanded a search for Volfe, which further revealed the barely controlled chaos that existed on all levels. In the meantime, Coffer consolidated her position. Captain Darsen was safely in custody—and under sedation—in MedSec. Dr. Kervatz reported his state as remarkably calm, considering. Indeed, the news that they had passed through the rift brought a marked smile to his face. Or so Kervatz said.

After an hour more of hard work, Coffer began to believe that everything was as under control as she had indicated it was long before to the crew. Being pragmatic, Security had long since given in.

The search for Volfe, however, revealed that she had been killed in one of the spates of fighting following the take-over.

Someone else Coffer could trust would have to be placed in charge of the chart room.

"How about Mora Elbrun," suggested Norlan.

"I completely forgot about her," said Coffer. "I hope she's still alive . . ."

At one time—perhaps when she had joined the Space Service—she had believed that there might be a point to her life. Now it seemed to her as though if indeed some god had previously mapped out the course of her existence, it had been a cruel and malignant one.

I seem to go through life losing people, she thought. My parents, Div, Ston . . .

Abruptly, she realized that she didn't know what deck she was on. Or what corridor in that unknown deck, for that matter. She had simply been numbly wandering since she had awakened, since she had visited Ston's badly burned and torn body, down below the sensor platform.

She seemed to be on a lower level—but beyond that, she wasn't sure.

Judging by the curvature of a concentric corridor, she headed toward the center hub of the deck. What with the unusual lack of activity here she could hear the hissing breath of the ship's air circulators; she even fancied she heard the thrumming heartbeat of the engines. In her shocked state she imagined herself the sole survivor of the revolt, alone in the guts of this cold artificial world.

"Are you okay?"

The voice startled Mora. She turned. A young man in an ensign's uniform was walking up behind her. Concern shadowed his features.

"You need some help—are you hurt?" he asked, stretching out his hand to her. How young. Unlined brow. Open face.

"You'd better get away from me," Mora said. "I don't want to know you."

"You're Mora Elbrun, aren't you?"

"No."

"You'd better come with me," the young man insisted. He sounded nervous. She was too drained of energy to resist when he took her arm. "Captain—Coffer—sent me to look for you. I'm taking you to MedSec."

"Of course."

"Do you know what's happened?"

Mora shook her head.

"We're through the rift—evidently way beyond our galaxy." He held her arm firmly as he walked her to a lift. "The mutiny is over. We won—that is, the mutineers won."

"Coffer is captain?" Mora sighed as she stepped onto the lift. "For some reason I thought only the children had survived."

"I'm not a child."

As the lift began to move up its chute, Mora looked at him again and began to cry.

"Well, she's in good condition and responding quite well to our psychiatric tests," said Dr. Kervatz to Coffer. "She's had a bad shock, but she's still in one piece." Coffer nodded absently, preoccupied with the bridge's vu-tank. She sighed, leaned back in her chair, and gave the doctor her full attention.

"However . . ." she prodded.

"However, she's listless. She lays in bed. She speaks rarely, usually only when spoken to. She's . . . disinterested."

"I see," Coffer said. "Perhaps if she had an assignment, it might prove, ah, therapeutic?"

"Perhaps."

"Good, because I have one for her. Look at the vu-tank, Doctor."

Kervatz looked and saw the thing that Coffer had been brooding over for two days. Shortly after braking the *Pegasus*' headlong rush into intergalactic space, the sensors had picked up what seemed to be a homing signal from a nearby dark object. Following it, they had found the rift station.

It could be nothing else, floating here so close to the rift, so far from any world. The size of a small planetoid itself, the station was a sphere made up of open metal webwork surrounding a much smaller, denser core. It was a gigantic, complex construction; what purpose could it serve here other than to monitor and perhaps *generate* the rift?

"I'm impressed," said Kervatz. "It looks like you could sail the *Pegasus* right into it, past the latticework and right to the—"

"You could—if you were crazy," Coffer said, cutting him off. "That thing is putting out hard radiation. A human being wearing the best protective pressure suits we have on board could safely remain in that place for maybe eight hours."

"Nasty," Kervatz agreed. "But that wouldn't worry you unless you intended to investigate anyway."

Coffer was surprised. "That's true. We're low on raw supplies—chemicals, foodstuffs—"

"I should think the casualties would cover at least a portion . . ."

"Watch it," Coffer snapped. She lowered her voice. "The less the crew thinks about that, the better. At any rate, we can't afford not to investigate the station.

"I want to send a shuttle with five people on board to that place. Not only for possible procurement of supplies, and simple curiosity—maybe we can get hold of some information on the rift itself. Just because we made it through this way doesn't mean it operates both ways. I want to make sure. Anyway, you'll have to wear specially prepared suits."

"What do you mean *you'll* have to—" said Kervatz, disconcerted.

"We'll need constant on-the-spot monitoring of the radiation hazards inside the station, performed by a medically competent individual," Norlan explained. "Of course, if you'd care to recommend a qualified subordinate—"

Kervatz glowered at him. "I thought it was customary to ask for volunteers in this sort of situation."

"Don't be romantic. Now, do you think I should assign Mora to this?"

"After what she's been through? She seems to have been quite attached to that Ston Maurtan fellow."

"It'll give her something to do, to think about," Coffer pointed out. "Further, she knows more about *Tin Woodman* and Div Harlthor than anyone else. And her Talent might come in handy."

"You're really certain the rift and *Tin Woodman* are directly related?" Kervatz asked.

"Aren't you?"

Kervatz shrugged. "Does Mora get a choice about this?"

"Yes. Next question?"

"Why don't *I* get a choice?"

"You were a neutral during the fighting," Coffer said quickly. Then she smiled.

"Bitch."

"Captain Bitch to you, Doc. Ask Mora if she'll go. With or without her, the shuttle will launch at 1600 hours."

Kervatz shrugged and rang MedSec through the intercom on Coffer's desk. "Is Mora Elbrun awake?" he asked.

"Yes, sir," answered Ensign Harris, the young medical technician who'd responded to the call. He sounded strangely nervous. "But, Doctor—"

"Fine. I want to talk to—what's wrong?"

"We have a problem—a missing patient—"

"Not Mora?" Kervatz asked.

"No, sir," Harris replied, swallowing hard. "Captain, I mean, Mister, uh, I mean—Edan Darsen, sir. He's gone."

Coffer swiveled in her chair and pushed Kervatz away from the intercom. "This is the captain. I thought you had Darsen under control down there—what happened to Security?"

"I—we guess that one of the security people helped him, or just let him walk away," Harris replied. His voice was faint.

"Great." Coffer cut off the intercom. She and Kervatz stared at one another in bewilderment for a moment. "Well, we'll just have to organize a search for him," she sighed at last.

"Do you think he can do any harm now?" Kervatz said.

Coffer shook her head. "No. In fact, I wonder if he isn't—" She stopped. It was better not to speculate on Darsen's state of mind; she would simply wait and see what happened.

It didn't take long for Security to find Edan Darsen. He had gone directly to his own quarters, discarded his MedSec smock, and put on his seldom-used gold dress uniform. Apparently whatever security person who had been loyal enough to Darsen to help him escape had also lent him a hand laser.

It took a three-man work detail several hours to clean up Darsen's quarters. They placed his headless body in a plastic bag and took it to the hangar deck and ejected it into space without much ceremony.

Mora was eager to leave the haunted corridors of the *Pegasus*, if only for a few hours. She had agreed to join the expedition team, though she had no idea what useful purpose she could serve.

The others aboard the shuttle with her were specialists. Dr. Kervatz would monitor the station's radiation and its effects upon them —and was nominal leader of the group. Melanie Wellow was a civilian biochemist, a member of an exploration mission which the *Pegasus* had been transporting to its destination. Ensign Freitag was a physicist, and Lieutenant Sauk was a structural engineer.

As the shuttle passed through the rift station's outer structure, Mora couldn't help feeling like a fifth wheel.

This station, with its giant bare metal skeleton, glowing lights, and dangling cables resembled a crazy cosmic carnival ride. Mora could see things which looked like seats: concave plates attached to the structure at regular intervals. As the shuttle passed close to one of these, Mora saw that it was almost as big in circumference as the *Pegasus* was long.

"Those aren't structural beams," Freitag announced, regarding the others owlishly. "Those metal parts which ring the station, I mean. They're cylindrical in cross section; probably tubing."

"Why tubing?" asked Sauk.

"Just a guess," Freitag admitted, adjusting and rechecking his suit as he spoke. They had put them on before launching—the shuttle was too confined for the maneuvering needed to don suits of the sort they wore. "I'm assuming that the outer shell of the station is a functional part of the rift-generating apparatus. Maybe they just hold coolant fluids—or perhaps they have plasma pumped through them at high velocities. . . ." He rambled on through an increasingly esoteric series of speculations concerning the nature of the rift generator, which Mora found incomprehensible.

"What are those big, curved things like seats?" she inquired at last.

Freitag shrugged.

"Docking rests for other creatures like *Tin Woodman?*" suggested Sauk. "This place is built on a scale suitable for such creatures."

The plural struck Mora. She had always assumed that there were, somewhere, many creatures like the one which had taken Div. But Sauk's remark and the sight of the rift station brought new understanding and imminence to the idea.

"The inner core is coming up," Kervatz announced, watching the navigation display console. "I hope this goddamn ship knows how to stop itself."

"Coffer knows," Mora reassured him. "She'll take over control from the compilot by remote."

The inner core of the station was a solid walled sphere which could hold thousands of ships the size of the *Pegasus*. Under Coffer's apparent control, the shuttle slid around the circumference of the sphere in a tight orbit until it reached a circular recess of about ten meters' diameter in its surface. "I guess Coffer thinks this is a door," commented Kervatz. "Do we knock?"

"Use the shuttle's lasers," said Sauk. "This has to be a sort of airlock. You can't expect that the inhabitants would suit up and evacuate the air from this whole thing every time someone entered."

"If indeed *Tin Woodman*'s race built this, why would they need air?" asked Wellow.

"Perhaps they can operate in both. In space, certainly, they must have to generate some sort of inner atmosphere," said Sauk.

Then the lasers licked out at the door. Evidently Coffer had reached Sauk's conclusion independently. The twin beams slowly drilled a four-meter hole in the metal surface.

"Everyone have their jets on?" Kervatz asked. "Good. Check your oxygen. And once you're outside the shuttle's shielding, for God's sake, don't stop to gawk." He stole a glance at the radiation meter on his left wrist. "This part of the station is cooler than the rest, but that's not saying much. We've got four hours inside, with an hour's

safety margin. Remember that we have to get far outside the outer
station before we're in the clear.

"Move it!"

The shuttle's pumps sucked the air from the cabin. The doors
opened, and the five explorers jetted out, steering for the hole in the
station's skin. Mora was last. As she reached the interior of the
airlock, Sauk was examining the inner door of the huge cylinder.

"The lock seals automatically when the outer door is punctured,
of course," he announced. "Call Coffer and see if she can focus the
lasers on the inner door through the hole in the outer one."

"You'll kill anyone that might be inside!" protested Wellow.

"I don't think there's anyone in there. They'd have given us some
sort of indication if so," countered Sauk.

Kervatz established communication with Coffer and explained the
situation. Coffer told them to flatten themselves against the airlock
wall furthest from the puncture—several minutes later the shuttle's
laser flashed, drilling a hole smaller by half than the first one into
the inner door. There was no explosion of escaping air.

"Not pressurized in there," said Freitag.

"This place has been a ghost for a long time," Mora returned. She
could *sense* it. Now, drawn by curiosity, she took the lead. She jetted
through the hole before its edges were completely cooled.

The interior of the station was different from anything she had
imagined. As the others, one by one, followed her inside, they too
were silent, stunned.

Sauk finally broke that silence. "I thought it would be designed like
a starship," he said. "With enclosed levels, rooms . . ."

It was not. The greatest area of the sphere was one vast, open
space. There was no appreciable gravity, strangely. Mora began to
feel slightly ill. The dark void of space was unfathomable to her
senses; the rift station had a sense of scale which space lacked. She
felt as though she were high above a city, falling.

The walls were lined with tens of thousands of compartments, like
small dwellings but open to the gaze of an outsider. On the far side
they resembled a hive or skyscraper built by a mad architect who had
never felt the deadening clumsiness of gravitation, nor known the
human need for privacy. Lights blazed from many of these compartments, though Mora saw no movement in any.

Throughout the open space many objects drifted. Some were simple featureless geometric forms in bright colors; others resembled

smaller versions of the wall structures. They moved freely about the station, their motion apparently random; yet no two collided as Mora watched.

"I hope someone left blueprints lying around here," said Kervatz.

"I suppose you want them in English," joked Freitag.

"Perferably."

"Well, I'm no use to this mission," Wellow announced. "This place has probably been deserted since before Earth's last ice age. Even if the inhabitants had consumed food that we could use, I doubt there's any chance we'll find it intact."

"Look at that one building near the center of the sphere," said Freitag. "It hasn't moved. I don't think so, anyway."

"How can you tell?" asked Kervatz.

"No, he's right," said Mora. "I've noticed it, too."

"It could be a control center," Sauk mused. "We might find what we're looking for there."

"Do you realize how far away that is?" Kervatz objected. "Over fifty kilometers! Just getting there and back on these jets would take over an hour. And we could easily get lost."

"No," Mora said. "If two people stay here at the opening, I think I could guide us back. There's a limit to my Talent, but with so few of us here, I think I could sense my way toward someone pretty well."

"You think. What if you're wrong?" Kervatz demanded. The sudden babble of four voices all arguing into his radio seemed to be worse than any other fate Kervatz could imagine. "What the hell," he relented. "Wellow, Freitag—you stay here. If we're not back in two hours— No, scratch that. I expect you two to wait nobly for us until you rot in your suits. No reason *you* should get off easy."

Mora, Kervatz, and Sauk set off for the central structure, steering themselves by visual judgment alone. This was not too difficult, since the lack of atmosphere caused even distant objects to stand clearly defined; but it did demand considerable concentration.

Distance had deceived them however. When finally they reached the "control center" it was far larger than they had assumed, comprised of many open chambers and extending for hundreds of meters in all directions.

"We still need a map," groaned Kervatz.

"Head for the center," said Sauk. "It seems logical, considering the design of the station."

"How?" asked Mora.

"Well, all the other free units actually orbit this thing. Everything is built around a point. It may even be . . . it may be that the station was built around a preselected point in space because it was necessary for the rift's functioning."

"May as well try." Kervatz sighed.

The three of them moved into the control center.

"Captain, we have a problem," Lieutenant Cushnam reported.

Coffer walked from her command monitors toward the sensor station. "What is it?"

"Since the exploration party entered the station's core, radiation levels there have started to rise. It was minimal at first, but if it keeps increasing at its present rate . . ."

"Kervatz is in charge," Coffer interrupted. "He'll—no, better inform them anyway. Who knows what's happening in there." She turned to Garyve at the communications console. "Send a message to the—"

"Captain," reported the communications officer. "I'm sorry, but our communication with them has just been jammed."

Coffer pondered. "We must have hit some sort of burglar alarm." She felt responsible—and lonely—as only a commander of others can feel. Her every decision affected the crew—and she hadn't been doing very well, from the mutiny onward.

"Leana, why did they—*Tin Woodman*'s race—build the rift station?" Norlan asked Coffer.

"I don't know," she said. "What difference does it make now?"

"I—I was just wondering. You know, no living creature could survive constantly increasing radiation like that. What kind of station is so desperately important that it's designed to kill its inhabitants to prevent take-over by an enemy?"

Coffer had no answer.

This room had to be the control chamber—Mora was certain of it. It seemed to be patterned after something familiar—something Div had shown her in their brief, last-moment contact: an ovoid of soft, resilient material, warm pastel in color. There were resting structures which vaguely resembled chairs scattered around the room. Ranged in front of the chairs were what appeared to be instrument panels without keyboards or any other visible means of operation.

In the center of the room floated a dark, featureless globe only slightly larger than a human head. Mora rocketed toward it. She chinned her transmitter. "I've found the main control room, I think." Kervatz and Sauk were close behind her, in the outer corridor. Not waiting for them to arrive, she reached out, instinctively, to touch the globe.

At her touch the globe seemed to grow. Her vision reeled; she seemed to fall forward toward the center of the thing. The outer world fell away, and on all her sensory levels she received a communication.

The history of *Tin Woodman*'s race passed before her like a filmed epic pageant.

And she understood. . . .

. . . and then Mora found herself abruptly conscious, floating in the center of the rift station control system and clutching the dark globe. Kervatz's voice crackled in her radio: ". . . radiation in this place is rising. I should have noticed it earlier. We have to leave, now! For God's sake—Sauk, see if you can pry her off that damned thing."

"No!" Mora shouted as hands locked on her wrists, pulling her away from the globe. She pushed the man away and moved back to the globe. She held it tightly in her hands. Nothing. The globe remained dark, silent.

"Mora, please." It was Kervatz again, his voice soothing now as he pleaded with her. "We don't want to leave you here. We have to go or we'll all die here."

"Yes," Mora said at last, releasing the now played-out globe. "Let's get out of here."

RIFT STATION EXPLORATORY REPORT
REPORT SYNOPSIS
EXCERPTS RE: CONTROL ROOM, HISTORY STORAGE GLOBE
MORA ELBRUN, SOLE SOURCE

. . . here I shall attempt to place into words, for the benefit of the committee of researchers assigned to study the subject, a brief outline of the pertinent highlights perceived by me through the curious memory bank described above.

Although the experiences were not in words—images and extrasensory information, rather—later thought on the matter has crystallized the information into these basic truths:

Eons ago, in a distant galaxy now long extinct, there had existed a planet much like Earth, or Crysor. On this planet had evolved, in symbiotic fashion, not one but two sentient races: The Gom, huge elephantine creatures, and the Tuu, who resembled human beings in many ways. The symbiosis the two races evolved was necessary for survival. The alternative would have been constant warfare between creatures of unlike minds, decimating both populations. Having made this crucial twist in their development, the Gomtuu were able to avoid even such war as had been known on Earth, for when two linked but independent consciousnesses made every individual decision, the potential for excessive self-aggrandizement at the expense of others was severely limited.

In the earliest stages of Gomtuu civilization, the Gom willingly served as the beasts of burden; in turn the Tuu possessed the physical flexibility the Gom lacked. Theirs were the hands which built the Gomtuu cities, laying upon one another the great stones which the Gom would carry from the quarries. Intellectually, the two races came to specialize, so that neither was whole without the other. The Gom were philosophers, the Tuu, scientists, in a sense. The Gom perceived things holistically, they saw creation as a pattern. The Tuu were analytical, breaking all things down to their component parts for the sake of understanding.

The rise of a world-spanning, peaceful Gomtuu civilization was accomplished within but a few millenniums. When finally they had turned their thoughts to the exploration of space, they were technologically and emotionally prepared to weld their symbiosis more tightly than ever: The Gom were developed, by genetic engineering, into space-going vessels in which their Tuu partners could live. The Gom were outfitted at full growth with their stardrives and what other mechanical parts were necessary to their function. They became cybernetic organisms.

The Gomtuu thus dispersed throughout their home galaxy, exploring and colonizing myriad worlds. The process wasn't without accident, however. In one new star system which was colonized, a virulent disease was encountered. The disease was invariably fatal, but selective in its chosen hosts: it killed Gom. Within two generations the Tuu of this colony were alone.

Without exception the Tuu of this colony went, by Gomtuu standards, mad.

The rest of the Gomtuu were unaware that this had occurred. Inevitably their new freedom and closer meshings with one another had eroded their need for society. Each pairing of Gom and Tuu so satisfied the emotional needs of its partners that the dispersal of the race became wider and sparser. Within a few thousand years the new colonies they had so boldly established became little more than hatchery worlds, where young Gom and Tuu were born, paired, and prepared for flight. No one noticed the disappearance of certain pairings.

But on that lost colony world, the insane remnants of the Tuu began to build their own society. They learned quickly to grope after what they wanted. They learned to kill one another for what they needed. Their brilliant analytical minds allowed them after long centuries to develop a scientific technology based on the dissection of corpses and the tearing apart of atoms. They stripped their planet, leveling mountains and diverting rivers.

The memory of the Gomtuu remained, as a belief in gods and demons. As the Tuu became more convinced that there was nothing their own ingenuity could not provide the answers to, the gods became to them only a particularly insidious form of demon.

The longing to return to space hung on also, as an irrational impulse among the Tuu. In time they did so, in bulky mechanical parodies of their ancestors' partners.

Inevitably, when the Tuu encountered the Gomtuu, war raged between them. Gomtuu hatchery worlds were destroyed by the Tuu. In desperation the Gomtuu reconstructed what had happened, forced themselves to band together once more as a species, and made what for them was a near-unthinkable decision: they immolated the Tuu home world. Their action was too late, for the Tuu had established themselves on thousands of the Gomtuu hatchery worlds. The war went on.

Finally, rather than continue a fight which they were not constitutionally capable of winning, the Gomtuu had constructed the rift station, with the intention of using it to disperse even more widely over the universe, and thus escape their enemies. . . .

Acting Captain Coffer put Mora's full report down and looked at the woman. "I find this very hard to believe. And that was the end of the recording—the construction of the rift station? You didn't get any information at all on whether it's safe—or even *possible*—to re-enter the rift. From the sounds of it, if we don't do it properly, we might end up in some *other* galaxy."

"I'm afraid that was all," said Mora. "I suppose we'll just have to risk it, unless we want to try to find some inhabitable world around here—which doesn't seem likely." She met Coffer's stare across the conference room table. Ranged about them were the other members of the mission, as well as the appropriate experts on the subjects under discussion. "And I should have added this to my report; I've been thinking about it all, over and over—the Tuu. I wonder if maybe Earth wasn't one of their colonies—perhaps that would explain why there are human beings on Deva and Crysor."

"Are you suggesting," said Kervatz, eyebrows raised, "that these so-called Tuu are the source of the human race—indeed were humans themselves?"

"I'm not sure *what* I'm suggesting, Doctor. Perhaps humans are some special mutation or breed of Tuu, suited to our sort of worlds. At any rate, at this point of development, humans and the Tuu would be practically alien anyway. Certainly humans would be alien to the Gomtuu.

"And I can't help but wonder—*Tin Woodman* was found pretty close to the Triunion worlds, considering the distances involved. On its way to these Tuu colonies for some special mission . . . ?"

". . . or on its way *back?*" finished Norlan. "Questions, Mora. Interesting, true, but a far cry from facts."

"I wonder what that mission was," said Mora softly to herself. *Or is?*

They were in the middle of feasibility investigations as to the repenetration of the rift, when twenty objects jarred the sensors of the *Pegasus* into action. Twenty objects that at first were simply small lights in the visual screens.

These glowing objects halted just beyond deflector range. The captain, elsewhere on the ship, was immediately notified. The first thing she did when she got a look at the readouts on the objects from the sensor banks was to call Mora Elbrun up to the bridge.

As she stared in disbelief at the magnified images of the objects, Mora felt a tide of awe and wonder wash over her—and anticipation as well. She had not expected this. And yet she welcomed it as though she had been waiting for it all the while.

There was no doubt in her mind. *Tin Woodman* was out there, with its fellows, notified of their presence by some signal transmitted when they'd entered the rift station.

Div had returned.

SEVENTEEN

"Switch the deflectors down to small objects only," commanded Coffer. Her eyes remained on the blobs of light glowing in the primary view screen.

"Do you think that's wise? How do you know they don't intend us harm?" said Norlan. "After all, we've pursued *Tin Woodman* across the universe. It might not wish us to return with the news of the space rift."

"No," countered Mora. "No. We have nothing to fear." Something . . . something in her was reaching out to the new arrivals—and something in her told her that they were reaching out to her as well. She strained to touch it, realizing it was too far. Like trying to touch a star . . .

"I don't know," Norlan responded nervously. "Why the other ships, then?"

Lowering her voice, Coffer said, "I don't know. But their very presence indicates we'll find out quite soon. If they intended violence, they'd not have approached us in this manner."

Even as the deflectors were adjusted, the alien ships drew closer. Soon their number filled the screen. All were similar to the form the crew of the *Pegasus* had discerned in the drifting vessel designated *Tin Woodman*. But the alien had been half-dead then, dormant. Now, if indeed it was among this fleet of its fellows, it fairly glowed with life, radiating an astonishing steady pulse of energy. The sensors were swamped with new information.

Within half an hour, the fleet of aliens was less than twenty kilometers away. Here all of them stopped save one, which ventured another ten kilometers closer to the *Pegasus*. It halted finally, hanging in space before them. They could see every detail of its hull. All the while Norlan had been attempting to communicate with the creature on some frequency, without success. "It would appear that when it wishes to speak to us, it will," he noted. "No way to raise it."

Activity all but ceased on the bridge. Every member of the crew could barely resist the impulse simply to stare at the wondrous luminescence the ship-being gave off.

Mora felt herself falling into a trancelike state of mind. All time seemed to fall off her, like discarded clothing. All the pain of the past seemed to lose its constant resonance—she seemed to be turning away from it, away from her troubled present, its scabs flaking, fading away as she pointed her psyche toward an anticipated future. It was like a soothing balm, a sweet forgetfulness. She was only vaguely aware of the others about her.

Sometime later, Div appeared.

Or rather, Mora could see, a projection of what Div had been. It began as a faint tremble of blue light spotted with pinpricks of green and yellow that burst into existence at the very center of the bridge, some two meters above the floor. It dashed a milky sort of glow into every part of the room—all eyes were drawn to the hypnotic effulgence that was suspended in the air like a tiny, cold sun. The light grew, slowly, into a large globe. Quivering, this light began branching streamers of itself outward—like pseudopods growing from an amoeba. There were five of these streamers. The lower two descended to the floor, assuming the shape of legs. The middle two thinned out into arms. The topmost bulged into an ill-defined head. Slowly, the image resolved into the recognizable shape of a human being, as though it were being focused into clarity inside a vu-tank. A soft glow still haloed the specterlike presence. The image resolved into a vague opacity. Mora could see through it with no difficulty. The slow dazzle that was the head slowly faded into features. Eyes, nose, mouth. Chin, ears, hair.

Div's mouth was set in a slight smile. His eyes glimmered welcome. The sheen he emanated carried with it a comforting tingle. Mora, peripherally, could feel that whatever fright the awe-struck crew had felt at this unannounced arrival was rapidly diminishing.

Div motioned with his hands, and it was as though he were casting his thoughts to the crew.

You have come, as I hoped you might. As I planned. It is well that you are here. This pleases us.

"What?" Coffer immediately assumed the role of spokesman for the group. "You mean, you expected us? How did you know?" Of course she was not used to telepathic communication. The thoughts that Mora received were pregnant with so much more meaning than the surface word/symbols indicated. She understood.

I essentially summoned you after me—there were things you had to see, experiences you had to have before you could understand the message I have for humanity. At the moment I speak to every individual on board the Pegasus, *completing the contact I instigated for the nanosecond before my Null-R jump. I am appearing before all of them, just as I appear before you. I have called you here because I still bear much love for the species that spawned half of my consciousness. You shall carry the message back to your fellows.*

We see that you have learned much of the history of our race. We are pleased. This is part of the reason I have called you here, so far from where we first met.

I might have lingered—but it was obvious that you were not yet ready for the message there was to give. Your commanding officers may well have been hostile—a factor which I was also instrumental in changing for our present meeting. Besides, it is best to show you rather than merely tell you. You have our history in your computer's information banks. You have documented proof. You shall need all this, later.

The image of Div held out its hands.

But to be understood, our story cannot be merely relayed in words and thoughts. You must understand its totality, its implications. And to achieve this, you must all be communicated to in different and diverse levels.

Div lifted his arms straight up. The contoured light which composed his body began to blur. Diamond-like scintillations began to sparkle as the body metamorphosed into a column. This coruscating cylinder began to spin, slowly at first, then faster. It narrowed at its base, became a cyclone of light which grew, its edges reaching out toward the surrounding watchers.

The river of light washed over *her* blinding *out all images of the bridge.* Mora, blinding her. She felt herself being drawn up out of her body by a soft, insistent pull. She did not resist, letting it tug her up into a greater light—such a light that nothing else seemed to exist. Then, perfumes whispered about her, calling her name in sounds made of scents. A wind *She splits into sensations and thoughts —thoughts that flow fast and thick, quite separate from the great lights perceived through synethesia. Her memories spiral out of their hiding places paying no heed to the order of their transpiring, but forming up before her in a crazy-quilt pattern that somehow weaves itself into something* bore her aloft and she floated like a kite suspended on breaths of music. The intense light began to swirl about her into colors too subtle for names. They pinwheeled joyfully above, stirring up the tender music into a fury that drew her up yet faster. Her senses were scrambled—her *quite beyond her previous interpretations of these experiences. Her childhood, her adolescence, her early womanhood—the memories spew on, some quietly, others rearing up as though to demand attention and reinterpretation. Most are painful, some recall happiness; but all vibrate with the insistent rhythms of life that she sees demand a song of meaning, to put them* mind fragmented, then reformed itself *into* a smoother, symmetrical whole. Suddenly, it turned topsy-turvy—instead of being drawn up into the center of the vortex, she fell down into it, fast.

She hit bottom, felt the essence of life enfold her as though she had pierced through its outer membrane of will, it somehow piercing her as well. There was a melding of spiritual juices that felt like tongues of cool fire licking at her soul. She surrendered to the pleasure/pain of it, and forgot what consciousness was.

When she awoke, she was no longer on the bridge. Nude, she drifted free in space. Stars and planets surrounded her like long-time friends. The void of space was no longer a cold, lifeless vacuum, but a sea of light that bathed her in soothing warmth. Light was life; life, light.

She was not alone. In the distance, alien life forms swam like schools of fish, grazing on the coronas of suns.

By her side was Div.

"Welcome to an experiential metaphor," he said. He too was nude. About them both, Mora could distinguish the tenuous outline of the being she had known as *Tin Woodman*. The name was now needless, ridiculous. "I am he, and he is I," said Div. "We are I; I am we. Yet I am still I."

"I can't—grasp . . ." she said. "It's beautiful, but I don't understand."

He laughed. The sound was of twenty laughs, blending together into a single effect—like the individual instruments of an orchestra melding. "I am no longer merely Div Harlthor, nor am I merely a combination of Div and the alien you call *Tin Woodman*. I am all of my fellows that hang here before your metal vessel. And yet, I remain Div Harlthor."

Gazing about, she saw the forms on the other ship-beings, each centered with its symbiote-rider. She looked back at Div. She shook her head, not comprehending.

He smiled.

They became . . . elsewhere.

On a seashore. In a tropical clime.

Mora found herself seated on a beach. Cool, frothy waves whispered up toward her, reaching for her, missing, falling back into the green-blue ocean. To one side of her, Div sat in physical form, drawing pictures in the gray and white sand. He looked up. He held out his hand. She took it in hers. It was warm.

"We waited for you, at my insistence. Soon, we shall depart this universe for one more suited for our existence. But I had them linger, for the sake of my parent race."

The huge orange sun, hazy on the horizon, was warm and pleasant on her bare skin. She leaned back into the hot sand. She watched Div. She held his hand tighter.

"First I shall explain. Then you shall experience," he said. "Just as in other places I am explaining to your shipmates."

"But how can you do this?"

Div shrugged. "How does one do anything that one does? It is not merely my power with which I speak to you, but that of all of us.

"As you may have concluded, the symbiotes were victorious in the war. As we grew, we abandoned our home planet for the greater freedom of space, learned to make that our home. Over the centuries we have developed not merely a double being—the space whale and its rider—but a singular being, the combination of all of us into one mind like the component cells of a brain."

"But how was that possible?"

"Your race bears the rudiments of the capability. In some it is greater than others. Over the ages, our race has developed it as well and uses it now for its ultimate purpose."

"You mean Talents? Like you—and me?"

"A poor name. But yes, that is what I mean. This is the reason I was able to link up with the alien—my Talent."

"The ultimate communication."

"Communication. Yes," said Div, staring out at the sea. A breeze frolicked through his hair. "From the moment it is separated from the intimate commune with its mother, does not a human child seek to re-establish this relationship—not only with its mother, but with its surrounding family of fellow humans? As it grows and falls deeper into itself, realizes its separateness from others, it also learns the methods of communication. Still, there is the constant inner war within it: the yearning for commune with its fellows against the ego it has developed as it has grown into an individual being.

"And yet, life would be impossible, unbearable, for an individual without the company of its fellows. Alone, any creature is insufficient. It is nothing without its fellows. Co-operation with them makes life viable, and even enjoyable. And one of the strongest drives in any sentient being is to communicate with its fellows.

"Take it further. If that is the case, then the ultimate communication is the intermeshing of minds as a whole. We approached that, Mora, just before I left the *Pegasus*. You felt a flicker of it when I transmitted that message just before dropping into Null-R space. That was also when I imbedded in all of you my Call. This is why you are here now.

"All of us ship-beings have strong powers of psi, which allow us to link together into what is effectively one mind, one consciousness.

"But the preservation of the individual is just as important, just as a chain is no more than a collection of individual links. Differing views of reality are necessary for species survival. Necessary for *love*.

"It is a delicate balance we have established. For if we creatures homogenize ourselves into one mind entirely, a mind without individual conscious entity components, then that mind is alone. And aloneness is intolerable in such an inhospitable universe."

"Why is it so important to tell us this? Why have you brought us here?" asked Mora.

Letting her hand go, Div stood, facing the sea breeze. "The human race has impeded its natural growth. They let themselves stand still. Their minds do not grow. They persecute those whose minds *have* grown. They wish to remain as they are—static. And thus they rot and wither on the vine of life. The universe will eventually slough them off. This I do not wish to happen." He glanced down at her, offered his hand once more. She accepted it, and he pulled her up to him. Placing her head against his chest, she closed her eyes.

When she opened them, they were . . . somewhere else altogether.

They stood on a cliff overlooking a much darker sea than before. Above the dark, choppy sea was a clear blue night sky, laden with stars and bright moons and color-streaked planets. A cool wind pounced on them. Div held her close.

"We are alone now, Mora. I speak only to you. The others of the *Pegasus* are back in their mortal bodies. I have placed specific instructions on the method of returning through the space rift. Soon my people and I will leave."

"Why only me?"

Div kissed her forehead. "Experience, Mora Elbrun. Experience my present existence, then dream my dream for mankind."

She was falling.

The scene jerked away from her, and she was falling a measureless distance across the span between minds. Falling into Div.

When the descent halted, she was Div as much as she was herself. Here the contact was yet deeper than the previous one experienced with him. She knew every nuance of his soul, every highlight and low point of his pain-streaked earthly existence. She participated in a replay of his trip into the ship-being. The combining of minds. The ecstatic brief contact with the humans aboard the *Pegasus*, the seeding of his designs in the necessary minds, the journey to rejoin his fellows. Through all of this, she knew *Tin Woodman* as well, and the creature welcomed her. When the fleeting finish of the experience arrived she knew what it was to be a part of a mass mind—and yet remain an individual. It was breath-taking. She had never felt so close to creatures, nor felt so strong the bond of love between them.

Then, like the shattering of a fragile crystalline bowl, she felt her mind seem to burst, sending its sparkling shards tumbling through canyons of time. Each of the myriad pieces flung helter-skelter through the universe was a part of her, intimately linked with the others through the enigmas of time and space. Stars were so many glittering specks in the sweeping beach of infinity, girded with an ocean of nothingness. Death and life seemed meaningless words; cyclic states. She sprinkled a part of herself through a globular galaxy, breathing in suns which smelled like crushed buttercups. The songs of the dimensions beyond her haunted her ears in vague alien tunes. A shower of comets landed on her metaphorical tongue like falling snowflakes.

Jarringly, she cohered into a whole once more, instantly realizing that she was more than before. Her fingers glowed with fine webworks of glittery thread; her body was covered with a soft, pliable sparkly gauze.

Div was beside her; she knew it, though she could not see him. "Experience us, Mora."

The last curtain of his mind dropped, sheared off from the top. She stared into his naked soul, and beyond into the souls of twenty others. Not like Div—she could see their alienness now. But they were alive, and life was what counted. They were alive and combined, like organs in a body, efficiently complementing one another in the composition of the whole—yet full individuals on their own. She felt a wash of warm raindrop love splash about her—and she was a school child again, plashing in a stormy park, synchronous with the world and herself. Instantly she yearned to hurl her lonely self into this mass of beings that knew no aloneness—only love, and security, and purpose.

In touching their minds, she experienced their history, saw their hopes, which branched out into places her mind was unable to go. It was as though she had journeyed through a chilling night all her life and now stood on the verge of dawn, the warm light of the Gomtuu just pinking the horizon.

It was gone.

Suddenly all became dark. Only Div was there, withdrawn.

"No!" she cried, a sense of deprivation she had never known before flooding her. She felt sick, empty, confused. "You can't take me away, after showing me this," she pleaded.

Div said, "This is not for you, Mora." There was a strange tone in his voice, an emotion straining to break through bars of control. "Believe me. No—these are not humans. I am not human, now." His pale form, outlined in cool fire, stood before her and lifted up its arms to touch her forehead. "What you have seen required eons of evolution among my new people. But let me show you my hope for mankind, Mora. Let me show you my vision. My dream."

And she saw.

She was on her back, sprawled on the floor.

. . . bridge . . . *Pegasus* . . . Gomtuu . . . Div . . .

Her thoughts were spiraling wildly down into her, disassociated. She felt disoriented. And then the thoughts ordered themselves, and everything was clear.

She lifted herself up, looked around. The others of the bridge crew were similarly prone, some beginning to stand. They looked confused.

Pushing herself the rest of the way up, she had to lean against the command desk. She found herself staring into the eyes of Leana Coffer. At first those eyes seemed in another place entirely; gradually they returned to focus, and the mind behind them realized that someone was looking into them.

Coffer attempted to speak. She produced only astonished, guttural sounds.

Mora helped her into the chair behind the desk. "Are you all right, Leana?"

"Yes. Yes." She shook her head, as though to clear it. "God, it was incredible. What—what I heard, saw, felt! The transmission from *Tin Woodman* before was only a glimmer of it. We *all* saw it. I could sense everyone there." She stiffened. "The Gomtuu. I must contact them before they leave. There are questions . . ." She began to move toward the vu-tank and flat-screen controls. Mora's hand detained her.

"They're already gone, Leana. We'll not see them again."

Coffer looked back at her in disbelief, shook off her hand, hurried to a control console, punching up all available visuals and sensor operations.

The flat screen snapped up before them immediately. Still hoping, she stepped up magnification, stared into the wealth of stars. But there was nothing there but the stars—and empty space.

Coffer sat down, defeated.

"So much to ask," she mumbled into her hands. "So much."

Mora went to her, smoothed a hand across her back comfortingly. "Then ask me."

Coffer looked at her. "What?"

The others who had awakened were staring at her as well. How she had hated that before: people looking at her, fixing her with mocking, unpleasant expressions of contempt. But now there was no contempt in those faces, no fear or suspicion. Only pure awe. And instead of despising those stares, she welcomed them. Before, they kicked up her self-doubt, her lack of self-assurance. They raked her over the coals of her insecurities, and the terrible emotions emanating along with them touched her mind like corrosive acid. But not any more. She would not be bothered, she realized, even if they still hated her. Because now everything was different.

"Div not only told me about the creatures. He showed me how it felt to be one of them. Can you imagine? A part of something as huge—full of love and promise—never alone, and yet remaining your-self? I find it hard to describe. It is the ultimate. But I can describe what Div showed to me—a vision of mankind's future with such verve and sweep it stunned me. And yet, it's possible. I saw it—and the very existence of the Gomtuu and their mind-mesh shows it to be possible!"

"What is possible, Mora?" asked Coffer.

"You all felt a part of the mind linkage, I'm sure. That is what I mean. That is what is possible."

"For the human race?" someone asked. "But how?"

She took a breath, let it out raggedly, emotionally.

"There are, among us, humans who are the keys to this ideal the symbiote creatures have achieved. In the very midst of the stagnant Triunion civilization, these people exist, and have existed for many years. And yet they are looked upon as freaks. They are hated and reviled. They are denied growth and maturation. They are feared.

"Div showed me his dream. I saw a mankind filled with love for one another. Not hate and fear. I saw masses of people that knew one another intimately and worked together for a common goal without division and strife among them. A civilization that existed not for self-gain, but for a mutual love.

"I saw a human panorama of unmatched splendor; a technology built not to serve itself, or just a few, but to serve the human ideal. I saw perfect cities on green planets with room to grow. And I saw human beings living together literally as one, in perfect peace.

"I should have to be a literary genius to construct phrases and sentences, metaphors, similes, and word-images of what I experienced. But I shall try. All my life, I shall try. And all my life I will travel among my people, trying to impart this vision to them.

"For you see, these human keys to this ideal future are none other than my own kind—Talents. And every human has the seeds of psychic energy. But these must be cultured, nurtured, encouraged as the years pass. There are things we can learn from my people—things beyond comprehension. For it is in the combining of minds, emotions, and spirits that we are making the inroads toward progress of the human mind—of human evolution.

"We are the hope of the human race. We who you have spit upon with your hearts should be loved for what we offer. We who have been outcasts so long, misunderstood, hated, feared by you Normals, are the chance for the human race to move toward what the Gomtuu have achieved. Because of our mental talents, because of our empathic faculties, we can teach you much. Study us. Duplicate what we have artificially, genetically, in your children. Honor *our* children.

"For the first time I feel comfortable with my Talent. It is a gift. Not a curse. Div has given direction to my existence. I have his message to carry to you, and to others. Far from being the *blight* of humanity, Talents are the only hope for the proper evolution and maturation of the human race."

She smiled a smile she never thought she could before—a smile that must mirror the new inner peace she felt. The bridge crew about her was silent, speculative.

"I have much more to tell you. But not now. There will be time. Right now, I must go and rest and think about this vision that Div and the Gomtuu have given me. I must decide how best to bring it to you, and to others."

Not actually realizing what she was doing, she coursed a warm flow of empathic love over all of them. They smiled at her, and she felt their feelings—good feelings—as well. Div had improved her Talent. Sharpened it.

As Mora turned toward the lift shaft, Coffer's words broke the silence Mora left in her wake. "No time to waste," Coffer said. "We've got the directions from Div. We've got to maneuver the ship to prepare to re-enter the rift. There's much to do. There's a long journey ahead of us."

Another voice objected, "But if we return, might we not be arrested as mutineers? Perhaps we should find some nearby Earth-type planet and colonize it. We have the necessary equipment."

Coffer's response was sharp and full of emotion. Mora turned, saw she was pointing at her. "I could give you a hundred reasons. But leaving us right now is the only reason that counts."

Mora smiled to herself. Such a strange thing to be loved. Such a strange experience to be a prophet, a bearer of a new message. A dull pain of memory touched her deep inside. If only Ston were here to share this with her.

But no. No more looking back to a past so fraught with pain and self-hate. For the first time in her life, she felt happy with herself—felt fulfillment. The future would by no means be easy. But each day would be a solid stairstep now to her heart's desire.

She stepped onto the platform, and lifted up to the observation deck to look at the stars, for the first time knowing her place beneath them.

EPILOGUE

In a spherical pattern, the nexus-link ship at the center, the twenty Gomtuu traveled through the mass of extradimensional energies that was Null-R space as one. The brilliant and blazing colors that boiled about them fell on inactive sensor receptors. All inner force was now focused on the nexus-ship, bridging the twenty various mind combinations, meshing the consciousnesses into a semblance of one. This communication exchange centered upon the recent experiential matrices built through their contact with the human ship. Empirical and metaphysical permutations were constructed to augment the stored group memory, so as to place it in the proper emotional/ situational context—so that it would be as much the truth to them in the future as it was then and would not suffer damage in transference to the mass memory system of the collective, so far away.

The entity named *Tin Woodman* by the humans hung at the very lowest point of the hierarchal levels. Even in size, it was not so large as its fellows. Once the separate vantage points on the experience were harvested, weighed, considered, and combined, the whole of the group-mind directed a specific, selective question to their fellow, who had been their spokesman, through the focus point of the nexus-link.

Brother, they said. It is complete. We have humored your desires because of your difference, which we must accept—and the acknowledged curiosity on our parts as to the progress of the human race, a onetime member of which now forms part of you. All is well, and we are well pleased with the new knowledge we may add to the collective. We rejoice as you must in our destination, after our separate journeys about this galaxy, surveying present conditions. We rejoice that you returned through the rift in time to make the journey with us. We anticipate the company of our fellows. Yet there is one aspect of this unusual contact which you instigated and controlled entirely, with only the aid of channeled energy from the rest of us, which puzzles us. What you told the humans, specifically the one you singled out—the one you have been so preoccupied with the time-periods we have spent waiting for the metal ship—what you let her experience: it is an untruth. We cannot comprehend—untruths have long since become almost alien to us. We are sure your human part must have been responsible. We have not obtained such an idyllic state, although it is what, as a race, we hope to obtain over the next few eons. Indeed, philosophers among us argue over it constantly, some claiming that such perfection is impossible. There can be no perfect combination of minds maintaining the separate identities of each cell member, they say. If we are totally one another, then we cannot maintain individualities. Wars have been fought—power struggles engaged in with the more powerful of our number who have attempted to suck us all into themselves. Ours is by no means the perfect and splendiferous existence you painted for the human. The extent and power of these imagined fantasies you showed her of ourselves impress us all, perhaps even inspires us to further investigation of the ideal. But why, brother, did you present it to the humans not as ideal, but as fact? This is needed for proper explanation to add to the rest of the memory matrix—and to satisfy our own interest.

The being that was *Tin Woodman* and Div Harlthor acknowledged reception of the query. It responded, The human race is decaying. There was a need to instill in them a hope and goal for the future. My symbiote-half has much interest in his former race. Much feeling. Integration is not yet complete between us; this has helped that.

But why, said the others, was the human woman picked out alone for the transference of these untruthful visions?

There was a long silence from *Tin Woodman*. And then: Because she bears the power that will effect a renewal in the progress of the human race. She has the power to contact minds, and can relate the vision I instilled her with to others of her kind.

It was obviously an incomplete answer, but the others let it suffice and proceeded to let their thoughts travel over other matters. Their new brother was a problem that would take a time to become accustomed to. He was welcomed, but he was different. They did not understand him. They did not comprehend this fierce emotion they now detected in him, and did not care to contemplate it now. It would slack off and die, surely. Until then, to touch it was like nothing they had experienced before. And so they avoided it, ignoring it and its source as best they could.

Keeping its place within the formation, *Tin Woodman* journeyed on through distance meaninglessly far from where it had orbited the double-star system, bereft of a companion, for so many ages. Within, its fleshy chambers fairly glowed with life. It was discovering itself again, and delighted in the exploration of every cell. The new part of it was especially fascinating, but very strange. But then, as soon as their consciousnesses were truly one, that would pass away. Now it reveled in itself, running through its chambers with its mind like a delighted little boy.

It was in its symbiote chamber now, the section that held the physical body of its new mind-half. Lit by the mottled, colored glows of the crystalloids embedded in room-flesh, the human was a wonder. This is a part of me now, it thought. I think now with its mind wrapped up within my ship-body. I am it. It is me. How marvelous.

It did not totally understand the reason it had kept its companions waiting by the space rift. Nor why it had said what it said to the humans. But somehow, it made it happy.

And yet all was not right. When it would journey to certain parts of its new mind, there were cold and lonely places, emptier than empty space. It had not been this way at first.

And that throbbing emotion that would boom out piteously, as though from a lost soul.

It avoided these chilling places of its new mind, for now.

They would warm up and fade away. Soon. Very soon.

He is almost fully covered now.

An arm pokes out. The tip of a foot, long since de-shod by the slow flow of connecting flesh. This new skin is translucent; the previous form of the human is just evident below it. Denuded, the boy's flesh is now punctured with the curling lengths of wire-like nerves and veins which will keep its functions continuous for many millennia.

And yet it is still recognizably Div Harlthor.

The head is covered by a cap of harder flesh, with viny tendrils piercing the skull. Part of this descends over the face, obscuring half of the features. But the left side is uncovered. The mouth holds itself in a relaxed state, the perfect moue of a content, sleeping baby.

But the eye—large, pink—is half open. There is a haunted, bittersweet look to that eye, frozen forever.

And down the cheek below it there is a tear track, which is slowly drying.